"You know what a man needs,"

Mitch drawled, "to live with you, Diana? Nobility of spirit ... And a whip and a chair."

He was blocking her exit. Diana looked down at his legs deliberately, but he chose to ignore her. "Leaving so early? The party's just getting off the ground."

"It seems to me that since you are supposed to be keeping a low profile, the smartest thing would be to stay in your room."

"I like to live dangerously." Mitch moved closer, so close their chests were almost touching. "There was a time you liked it, too, or you never would've gotten hooked up with me."

Diana felt the static lightning between them, hot and quick, making it impossible for her to breathe.

"So what do you say, Di?" Mitch asked huskily. "You still like to live dangerously?"

ABOUT THE AUTHOR

The versatile Rebecca Flanders is a familiar name to readers of American Romance. Since 1983, when she supplied the introductory sampler to the series, she has written over a score of American Romance novels. In addition, she's the author of romantic suspense, mainstream and historical romance novels. Rebecca makes her home in the mountains of Georgia.

Books by Rebecca Flanders

Don't miss any of our special offers. Write to us at the following address for information on our newest releases.

Harlequin Reader Service
P.O. Box 1397, Buffalo, NY 14240
Canadian address: P.O. Box 603,
Fort Erie, Ont. L2A 5X3

REBECCA FLANDERS

THE LAST REAL MAN

Harlequin Books

TORONTO • NEW YORK • LONDON
AMSTERDAM • PARIS • SYDNEY • HAMBURG
STOCKHOLM • ATHENS • TOKYO • MILAN
MADRID • WARSAW • BUDAPEST • AUCKLAND

Published March 1993

ISBN 0-373-16477-7

THE LAST REAL MAN

Chapter One

The riot in the lobby was, as far as Diana Moore was concerned, the last straw.

She knew it was going to be a bad day when she got out of bed an hour late that morning. On her way out the door the telephone began to ring and in her hurry to avoid it, she snagged her stocking on the climbing rose that decorated the wall beside her front door. She stepped in a mud puddle up to her ankle as she ran for the car, only to discover a flat front tire—even the Mercedes people, she supposed dryly, couldn't issue guarantees against that—forcing her to take a cable car to work. Though cable cars were not her favorite method of transportation, she normally wouldn't have minded, but it was raining, the cars were crowded and the result was one ruined silk blouse and one hopelessly damaged pair of Italian pumps.

And that was how she walked through the doors of the elegant St. Regis Hotel, wet, bedraggled, and an hour late for work, and stepped into the middle of a riot.

The lobby was filled with squealing girls. Flash-bulbs were popping, people were shouting, tough-looking men in black leather jackets were shoving and pushing. And in the center of it all, from what Diana could tell, was a tall young man—or perhaps woman—with long blond hair, dressed entirely in white.

She stumbled backward, pushed and shoved by the jostling crowd, and strained to get a glimpse of what was going on, with little success. Arthur Hollings, the assistant manager, burst out of his office, looking terrified and indignant. Griff Mercer, head of secu-rity, was running toward the front with his walkie-talkie at his mouth. Other security men began con-verging from all directions but didn't seem to know what to do. The guests who had been lounging quietly in the lobby, enjoying their complimentary morning coffee, surged toward the center of activity, adding to the confusion. The bell captain stood gaping, and so did the three on-duty clerks at the front desk.

Diana fought her way toward them and managed to catch the arm of Tim, one of the day bellmen, in the process. "What is it?" she shouted. "Who is that?"

The first part of Tim's reply was cut off by the sound of a vase filled with fresh flowers shattering on the marble floor and the resultant cries of alarm—or perhaps delight—that accompanied it. "—rock star!" Tim cried, his eyes shining. "Two limos full of bags! Mammoth tips!"

As he hurried to be among the first to place his hands on the bags, Diana saw her assistant, Elise, frantically waving to her from across the room. Wedging herself between the press of bodies, ducking to avoid flying articles of clothing, she managed to reach the concierge desk just as someone decided to enhance the atmosphere by turning on a boom box full blast.

"What?" Diana shouted to Elise, but the sound was lost in the drum beat of heavy metal.

Elise leaned over the desk and shouted in Diana's ear something that sounded like "Hot blood!"

"*What?*" Diana repeated.

"Jason Hotblood! The English rock star!"

As chief concierge and newly promoted director of guest relations, Diana was of course aware of the singer's impending arrival. But his reservation was for two weeks hence, and no one had said anything about *this*.

"But that's impossible!" she cried. "He's early! He can't just waltz in here two weeks early. Are you *sure?*"

Elise shook her head helplessly. "That's what they said!"

"*Who* said?"

"One of his bodyguards!"

"His *what?*"

"Those guys in the leather jackets—they're his bodyguards. Look—at the desk! There's one of them."

Diana stood on tiptoe until she saw the man Elise indicated. He stood with his back to them, wearing a black felt fedora pulled low on his head, black leather motorcycle jacket, jackboots and black-lensed glasses. It was impossible for Diana to hear what he was saying from this distance, but it was obvious he was giving orders. And from the awed look on the desk clerk's face, he was doing so with no small degree of authority. Diana began to make her way toward him.

There was another crash and the sound made Diana wince, jangling her nerves. She reached the desk just in time to hear the man in the leather jacket say, "—deplorable lack of security! You'd just better hope we decide not to sue! Now, get your people—"

Diana caught his arm and whirled him around.

Diana couldn't understand why she had not recognized him before she heard his voice. Even from the back, even with that absurd hat and what she could now tell was a costume-shop Vandyke beard, even in black-out sunglasses and jackboots, Mitch DeSalvo was unmistakable. Every part of him was burned on her brain.

He was a distinctive-looking man. He had a square face, olive complexion and brown-black eyes. Curly brown hair that always looked in need of combing; strong, blunt hands. He had a smile that could effectively interrupt the heartbeat of any woman within viewing distance and a way of looking at Diana that could turn the strong muscles of her thighs to jelly. He was the most arrogant, obnoxious, inelegant and infuriating man she had ever known. He was also the only man she had ever loved.

She jerked her fingers away from the crinkled leather of his jacket as though burned, and he lifted his hand to strip off his sunglasses. That grin of his started to work on her immediately. He leaned one elbow on the counter in a deliberately provocative pose that parted the material of his jacket over a chest-hugging white cotton T-shirt, thrusting his denim-clad pelvis forward in a way that, had any other man tried it, would have looked pretentious and absurd. On Mitch the gesture was entirely natural—and ridiculously effective.

His dark eyes moved over her in that slow lingering way that made her skin tingle, missing no detail. He started at her water-splotched shoes, moved up over her ruined stockings, stopped to caress the hem of her skirt in a way that caused Diana instinctively to press her knees together. His gaze searched out the shape of her hips and moved over the juncture of her thighs and across her abdomen, low, where Diana could feel the muscles tightening, and then slid slowly across her waistband and over her rib cage, seeming to cup the shape of her breasts beneath the silk blouse. Mitch looked at a woman as though he were tasting her.

There was amusement in his eyes as they met hers, taking in the strands of hair escaping from her bun, the anger in her eyes, the tightness of her lips— amusement and a certain, secret knowledge that infuriated Diana, just as though he knew about the dryness in her throat and the pounding of her heart and the helpless, maddening, totally instinctive hardening of her nipples—which, of course, he did. There was very little about her body Mitch did not know, a truth that frustrated and embarrassed Diana every time she was forced to confront it.

"Hello, sweetheart. You're looking a little frazzled. Bad day?"

Diana's fists clenched at her sides. It was with a very great effort that she kept her voice from shaking with fury. "You! I should have known you'd be behind this. Any little thing you can do to ruin my life, right, Mitch?"

"Darling, please!" He raised his hand in mock warning. "Lower your voice. I'm undercover."

"Under—" She caught the ragged edges of her temper with an effort but could not quite bring the timbre of her voice under control. "How am I supposed to lower my voice when I can't even hear myself think?''

Mitch raised his hand over his head and made a snapping gesture with his fingers. A second later, the booming sounds of heavy metal ceased. Diana stared at him.

"Are you responsible for this?" she demanded hoarsely. "Of course you're responsible for this! Who *are* these people? How *dare* you!"

Mitch affected a pained look. "Give me a break, sweetie. People are staring. The whole idea was to be inconspicuous."

"Inconspicuous!" Her voice was becoming shrill. "People who want to be inconspicuous do not start riots in the lobby of one of San Francisco's most prestigious hotels! They don't barge in here with motorcycle gangs and—"

"Riot?" Mitch lifted his eyebrows. "You call this a riot? Trust me, I know riots and this isn't one. A minor disturbance, maybe."

"How dare you do this? Who is that person?" She gestured wildly in the direction of the tall blond person in white. "What are you trying to pull?"

"You'd know exactly what I was trying to pull if you had answered your phone. I did try to warn you. It's not my fault if you—"

"Not your fault!" She was practically screeching now. She heard herself, she saw herself in the incriminating mirror of her mind's eye—wet, disheveled, red faced, screaming at a man in jackboots in the middle of the lobby of the St. Regis. She was appalled, but she couldn't seem to stop herself. Mitch always had that effect on her. As effortlessly as he shrugged his shoulders, he could reduce Diana Elizabeth Haversham Moore of the Boston Moores, product of seven generations of breeding, refinement and quiet unobtrusive wealth into a coarse, bug-eyed fishwife with the lung power of a banshee. Just knowing that plunged Diana into a state of impotent rage. "Nothing is ever your fault, is it? God forbid that you ever actually take responsibility for your actions. I'll have you know—"

"Ms. Moore, please." Arthur Hollings had made his way to the desk and now stood beside her. The expression on his face could have frozen fire. "I would think we have enough chaos at the moment without one of the hotel's own employees making a spectacle of herself before a guest. I find the fact that you—" he emphasized the word with a look that made Diana want to sink through the floor "—would engage in such behavior particularly disappointing."

"Yes, sir." Diana swallowed hard and held on to her dignity with both hands, determinedly keeping her eyes away from the amusement she could feel dancing in Mitch's. "You're right, of course, and I apologize. But this man is not a guest."

Arthur turned a curious look on Mitch. "Excuse me, but aren't you with the Jason Hotblood organization?"

"That's *not* Jason Hotblood," Diana put in firmly, and with a note of vengeful satisfaction of which she was not particularly proud. "As a matter of fact, I'd be very surprised if there even *is* a Jason Hotblood! This whole thing has been a hoax, right from the beginning."

"Of course there's a Jason Hotblood," Mitch interrupted with an impatient glance and just the right dash of contempt. "He's the hottest thing in heavy metal, you should pardon the pun. You really ought to get out more, princess. How else do you think I came up with the idea for this diversion? I read in the paper about his planning to stay here. That *is* a deplorable lack of security, by the way," he added to Arthur, and then grinned. "Art, my man. How've you been?"

Arthur Hollings's dignity was a carefully cultivated thing, honed to perfection and elevated after years of practice to an art form. The President of the United States would not have called him Art, and the expressions on his face—from confusion to shock to outright disbelief—were comical to watch. Carefully shielding his face with his hand, Mitch peeled aside one corner of the beard. The astonishment in Arthur's eyes deepened and turned to delight. "Is that—? Mitch? Mitch DeSalvo!"

Mitch repasted his beard and raised a quick hand for silence. "Incognito," he explained. "Actually, the lady is wrong about something else. I am a guest. I needed to kind of sneak in without too much fuss so I brought along a few friends to keep the press busy." He indicated the gang in the center of the lobby. "I hope you don't mind."

Diana stared at him incredulously. "Since when do you worry about the press?"

But Arthur was saying, "No, no, of course not. Happy to have you anytime, and don't worry for a moment—not a word will leave these premises of your stay here."

"Sorry about the mess," Mitch added with every appearance of sincerity. "Just send me the bill."

"Daily," Diana interjected hotly. "Bill him daily."

Mitch draped his arm companionably over Arthur's shoulder. Diana had never seen anyone touch Arthur before. "I'll be needing a suite, I don't know for how long, and if I could get up there by the service elevator, I'll call off this zoo."

"Of course, right away."

Diana couldn't tell whether Arthur's enthusiasm was genuine or simply the easiest way to get away from Mitch's friendly arm. He turned quickly toward the desk. "Kevin, the Oleander Suite for Mr.—"

He hesitated, and Mitch supplied, "Mitchell. John Mitchell."

Diana noted with some surprise that he was now affecting an entirely new alias. He already had a repertoire of over a dozen. "I don't believe this!" she exclaimed. "You just let him sail in here, start a riot and wreck your lobby? And instead of calling the police, you give him a suite? What about those people? Who are they, anyway?"

Mitch spared her a glance. "I don't know. Just some guys I picked up in North Beach. Don't worry, they've been paid. They'll leave in a minute."

"North Beach!" Diana echoed, appalled.

Even Arthur looked disturbed by that and it was he who touched Mitch's arm this time, urging him along. "We're all set, if you'll come with me...."

Mitch did, draping his arm once again over Arthur's shoulder as he confided, "Listen, man, I don't want to tell you how to run your hotel, but you know this is just a dress rehearsal for what it'll be like when the real Hotblood gets here. Maybe you should..."

"I don't believe this," Diana muttered. She watched as Mitch escorted Arthur to the service elevator, talking to him earnestly all the while. "I really don't believe this...." Just before the elevator doors closed, Mitch winked at her impudently and blew her a kiss. Furious color surged to her cheeks as she whirled and made her way back to her desk.

"The man is checking into the St. Regis!" she exclaimed under her breath. "He's actually going to get away with it—again! Son of a—!"

She bit off the word at the last moment, and Elise raised her eyebrows. Elise, second runner-up in the Miss Black America beauty pageant and a former photographer's model, had exquisite eyebrows, and they could convey astonishment, outrage, disbelief or censure with more class than anyone Diana knew.

"Whoa," Elise said. "The only time I've ever heard you use language like that was... wait a minute." Enlightenment slowly dawned as her eyes moved to the elevator by which Mitch had just left. "Was that—it couldn't be! Was it?"

"It was," Diana said grimly, shuffling the schedules on the desk with harsh, angry movements, "the most arrogant, conceited, slovenly, worthless male specimen to ever walk the face of the earth. He gives new meaning to the term Neanderthal. I don't know why they let people like him run around loose."

Elise gave her a mild and knowing look. "Kind of makes you wonder why you ever married him, doesn't it?"

Diana scowled. "I know why I married him."

This time Elise's eyebrow formed a delicate comma, barely a question. Diana answered shortly, "For the sex."

She snatched up her notebook and started for the department heads meeting, for which she was already late. To her relief, and as Mitch had promised, the crowd in the lobby was already beginning to disperse. Damn him, she thought bitterly. Four hundred hotels in the city of San Francisco and he had to pick this one! Why? To do what he could toward ruining Diana Moore's life, that was why. As if he hadn't done enough already.

"Better make sure somebody calls Housekeeping to clean up this mess," she said to Elise as she left. "And," she added pointedly, "have a bill for the damages made out right now and sent to the Oleander Suite. Hand-delivered."

As paybacks go, it wasn't much, but it was the best she could do on short notice.

MITCH HAD JUST finished stripping off the beard and scrubbing the paste off his face when the bill was delivered. He opened the door to the fresh-faced bellman and gestured him inside.

"From the front desk, sir." The young man handed him an envelope. "Also, I was instructed to make sure you have everything you need and to ask about your luggage."

"Luggage," murmured Mitch, stripping open the envelope. "That's what I forgot." Astonishment crossed his face as he scanned the bill. "Eight hundred and fifty dollars for a vase? Three hundred and eighty for flowers? Jeez, somebody sure saw you guys coming."

With a dry and thoughtful look he tossed the bill and the envelope on the cherrywood desk beside him. "This," he said, "has the unmistakable look of the work of an ex-wife."

He glanced at the young man, patting his pockets absently for the package of cigarettes that wasn't there. "What's your name?"

"Tim Anderson, sir."

"You know anything about women, Tim?"

Tim grinned. "Not nearly enough, sir."

"Yeah, you and me both," Mitch agreed, frowning as he discovered pocket after pocket to be empty. "One thing I do know, though. There's not a man alive who was ever better off with one than without."

Of course, that did nothing to explain why he had just flown three thousand miles only to run smack into the one woman who had caused him more pure misery than any other single person in his life. Knowing that only sharpened his frown. He could have picked any hotel in the city. He could have picked any city in the country—in the world, for that matter. So he'd naturally headed straight for the one place on earth where he was less welcome than he was in New York City. And in New York he'd almost been killed.

Delayed Stress Reaction, he decided, that's all it could be. The same kind of thing that made perfectly ordinary-appearing people step calmly in front of a speeding train or walk unceremoniously through a thirtieth-story window. Coming here had been sheer idiocy, a temporary aberration, but—the shadow of a smile flickered across his lips as he made the admission to himself—he had certainly done it in style.

The entire subject was too imponderable for a man who had not slept or eaten anything but airplane food in forty-eight hours, and it was not in Mitch's nature to spend too much time analyzing things he couldn't change. The fact was he was here and he might as well make the best of it. Besides, it had almost been worth everything to see the expression on Diana's face.

He thrust his hand into his jeans pocket and drew out a roll of bills, peeling a twenty off the top. "Listen, Tim, run down and get me a couple of packs of cigarettes, will you?"

"Of course, sir. What brand?"

"Doesn't matter. I don't smoke. I need some other things, too—toothpaste, toothbrush, razor."

Tim accepted the money with the nonplussed expression of one who is accustomed to dealing with all kinds of eccentricities. "The concierge desk will be happy to supply the toiletries, sir. Just push '3' on your phone."

The frown on Mitch's face turned slowly into a look of pleasured speculation as his eyes moved to the telephone. "Yeah," he murmured. "The concierge desk. That's what it's there for, right?"

"Yes, sir."

Tim hesitated, and Mitch should have known from the shy, cautiously eager expression that crossed the bellman's face what was coming next. "Excuse me, but . . . you're Sal Mitchell, aren't you?"

One corner of Mitch's lips turned down wryly as he began to empty the contents of his pants pockets onto the desk. "That's got to be the worst-kept secret in this city."

Tim's eyes lit up. "I read your latest book."

"I hope you paid full price." Mitch's tone was cynical but he was no more immune than anyone else to the adoration of a fan. He couldn't help adding, "They're making it into a movie, you know."

"Wow! That'll be great. That last scene, in the subway—man, it blew me away. Where do you get your ideas, anyway?"

Again cynicism tightened Mitch's lips. "Places I'd be better off staying out of, believe me."

Tim suddenly seemed to recall he was on duty. "Well, I just wanted to tell you what a pleasure it is to have you at the St. Regis. I'll be back in a few minutes with the cigarettes, and if there's anything else I can do, just ask."

"Just leave the cigarettes on the desk. I plan to soak in the tub for about two hours. And keep the change, I'm a big tipper. Spread it around."

Tim grinned and touched his forehead in a small salute. "Yes, sir."

As soon as the door closed behind Tim the fatigue took hold; Mitch was almost too tired to move. He couldn't decide whether to call room service, start in with the concierge desk, or head for the bathtub—or whether to forget all three and simply collapse on the bed. So for a moment he did nothing. He just stood where he was, gazing absently at the contents of his pockets that were scattered over the highly polished surface of the cherrywood desk—now all he owned in the world. A wad of cash and some coins, a wallet full of credit cards he'd be stupid to use. A comb, a ring of keys, a penknife.... It wasn't much to show for thirty-four years of living. But then, he wasn't much of a collector; that had always been Diana's specialty.

Diana of the Radcliffe accent and finishing school manners. Honey blond hair, porcelain skin and navy blue eyes that seemed to smudge when she cried.... And Mitch had had the opportunity to see her cry a lot. But he remembered other things, too. A white lace garter belt. Silk stockings. Diana never wore panty hose, and her legs... Mitch's throat dried up, just thinking about her legs.

She had a way of looking at a man that could make his blood boil, or freeze it to ice. And when she got mad, the things she said, the way she would say them, would make him wish she'd just pick up a knife and get it over with. She was the only woman he'd ever known who had made him sorry to have been born a man, and yet he could not recall ever having felt so alive as when he was with her. The Ice Queen. The Viper. He'd been crazy to come back here.

And yet... A slow, somewhat resigned smile touched his lips as he picked up the telephone and dialed 3. It was inevitable, of course, just as getting on that plane bound for San Francisco had been. And as long as he was here, he might as well enjoy his stay.

Chapter Two

Diana had been attending the weekly department heads meeting for eight months now. She still wasn't quite sure how she was supposed to act, and none of the other department heads seemed to know how to treat her. Was she a concierge who had been promoted above her station, or their social superior who had no business working anywhere, much less in a hotel in which she had once frequently been a guest? Though no one would ever put it into words, the truth was found in a little of both.

Diana Moore spoke five languages fluently and was conversant in three others. She was erratically educated, impeccably connected, and possessed of very few useful skills. But she knew where to buy silk in Florence and mink in Amsterdam, and in San Francisco she knew virtually everything and everyone worth knowing. Where else should she have ended up but at the concierge desk of one of San Francisco's most prestigious hotels? She was eminently qualified for the position she now held—as the management of the St. Regis knew very well.

When a prominent Mexican businessman booked a suite, it was Diana who suggested that white gardenias might not be an appropriate amenity for his room as they were considered a symbol of death in the Mexican culture. When a group of German manufacturers lost their interpreter at the last minute, Diana stepped in effortlessly to fill the gap. The management quickly saw that Diana's talents were being wasted securing theater tickets and dinner reservations, but it was another two years before they found a way to promote her without removing her entirely from the concierge desk. Thus was born the position director of guest relations, and a seat at the big oak table every Thursday morning.

Fortunately Diana was not the only one who was late for the meeting. Both the manager, Rolf Severenson, and Arthur, his assistant, were missing from their respective places at the table. Their absence, Diana had no doubt, was in some way related to Mitch, just as she was certain from the way the conversational babble in the room ceased when she came in that everyone had been talking about her—or rather, Mitch. She could feel her stomach start to burn in the old familiar way, reminding her to check the supply of antacids in her desk. It had been over a year since she had last seen Mitch, and she had had no reason to stock up since then.

"Good morning," she said pleasantly as she took her seat. The murmured replies and furtive glances only confirmed her suspicion: they *had* been talking about her. Her stomach tightened another notch as she casually opened her notebook and pretended to study her notes. The murmur of voices in the hall announced the arrival of Rolf Severenson and Arthur Hollings. Everyone sat a little straighter. Notebooks were closed, papers were straightened. The managers of the St. Regis ran a very tight ship indeed.

Rolf Severenson greeted the assemblage with an absent, "People," and Arthur echoed the greeting with a nod. Amidst a restrained chorus of "Good morning, Mr. Severenson" and "Mr. Hollings," the two men headed toward the coffee service on the sideboard. Severenson made it a point to look at Diana as he did so. Diana returned his stare impassively.

Rolf Severenson ran the St. Regis like a European luxury resort despite the fact that he had been the first one in his family to ever finish high school. He didn't like Diana, but he was proud of her in the same way he was proud of the genuine Louis Quatorze escritoire in his office. He maintained exacting standards for all his employees, which was why he had been repeatedly named one of the ten best managers in the country, but with Diana his demands were always just a little higher. Diana understood this and learned to anticipate it, which made her even better at her job.

Diana had not expected mercy from him today and he did not disappoint her. He spoke with his back to the table as he filled his coffee cup. "You are all no doubt aware of the disturbance in the lobby earlier this morning. You'll be pleased to know that the situation has been brought under control and was, for the most part, a false alarm." He turned, smiling thinly at Diana as he balanced the delicate cup and saucer in one hand. "But perhaps Ms. Moore should be the person to fill us all in on the details."

Diana could not have worked for Severenson for five years without being prepared for a moment such as this. And she couldn't even be angry with her boss for putting her in such a humiliating position; it was, after all, all Mitch's fault.

As all eyes swiveled to her, she addressed the group in a perfectly modulated tone. "It seems one of our guests decided to play a little practical joke by pretending to bring in the Jason Hotblood entourage two weeks early. The damage seems to have been minimal and the guest—who is now occupying the Oleander Suite—has already been billed. And yes, as many of you already know, the guest's name is Mitch De-Salvo, also known as Sal Mitchell, M. D. Salvo, Mitchell Scott and Penelope Forrest, among others.

He is presently registered, I believe, under the name of John Mitchell."

Severenson's smile remained fixed and unaffected. "Thank you, Ms. Moore, for that excellent report." He moved to take his seat at the head of the table, with Arthur on his right. "You did, however, leave out one important fact. Mr. DeSalvo has requested complete anonymity for the duration of his stay, thus, one would suppose, the use of an assumed name. I do hope the rest of you will be more conscientious of security than the director of guest relations has been."

Diana's lips tightened fractionally, but she said nothing. Griff, the head of security, cast her an annoyed look.

Severenson added mildly, sipping his coffee, "I also expect that, as director of guest relations, you will make every effort to see that Mr. Mitchell's stay here is completely satisfactory."

Rolf Severenson would never have stooped to double entendre; he didn't have to. Simply reminding her that her job performance would be rated according to Mitch DeSalvo's level of contentment was enough to swamp Diana with humiliation.

She did not, however, allow any emotion at all to show as she returned a small smile. "Of course."

Pulling in his chair with a quick, decisive movement that officially signaled the start of the meeting, Arthur announced, "Somewhat pursuant to that, and of particular interest to our head of security, we have decided to cancel the *real* Mr. Hotblood's proposed visit in two weeks.''

The muted exclamations, ranging from shock to dismay, might properly have been deemed a volcanic outburst from this usually staid group. *I suppose I'll be blamed for that, too,* Diana thought grimly. *Thank you, Mr. DeSalvo.*

Severenson held up his hand for silence. ''Shall we move on?''

It was apparent that more than one person at the table was not at all ready to do so, but Mr. Severenson's word was law. It took Diana a moment to realize that the stares directed at her were not accusing, but merely impatient, which was another example of how her entire equilibrium was destroyed when Mitch was around. Like the owner of a semi-housebroken puppy, she was resigned to taking the blame for every accident that happened, whether or not it was her fault.

Because the purpose of the weekly meetings was, in great part, to review the needs of and prepare for the arrival of VIP guests, Diana's report generally led off the meetings. For the first time since the entire De-Salvo disaster—as she had already dubbed it in her head—began, Diana faltered as, under the impatient stares of fourteen busy men and women, she fumbled for her notebook.

"Ashton Levingworth arrives tomorrow," she read at last, relief washing through her as she found the right page. Diana hit her stride as, immersed in the needs of other people, in charge of a world upon whose order and predictability she could effortlessly rely, she let Mitch DeSalvo sink to the very bottom of her mind where he rightfully belonged.

Choosing flowers, ordering wines, selecting small tasteful gifts that were designed to impress without appearing ostentatious—these things Diana was bred for.

The limousine company that had received two guest complaints in the past week—that, too, was easily handled. Dismissing incompetent underlings was a skill Diana had learned at her mother's knee. Planning a sit-down dinner for twenty on three hours' notice, arranging a seating chart for a luncheon for thirteen women when seven of them weren't speaking to one another—those things barely presented a challenge for Diana. But with Mitch DeSalvo she was completely out of her depth.

Mitch DeSalvo, rude, loud, effortlessly obnoxious, with an uncanny knack for turning up at the worst possible time and doing the most possible damage to Diana's carefully ordered, lovingly polished way of life. Mitch DeSalvo, who could ooze charm like snake oil when he wanted to and who always seemed to know just the thing to say to make a friend for life out of almost everyone he'd met. She would rather take on the entire League for Social Reform single-handedly than spend one hour trying to deal with Mitch. She would rather clean up the suite after the Los Angeles Dodgers held a three-day celebration party. She'd rather ...

"If that's all right with you, Ms. Moore."

Diana stared at Arthur blankly, only the pounding of her heart registering her alarm at being abruptly jerked back to the present. She had long since finished her presentation, the meeting had gone on around her, and she had no idea what she was agreeing to when she replied easily, "Yes, of course."

Arthur nodded and glanced around the room. "If there's nothing else then, we're adjourned."

Damn him, Diana thought as she gathered up her notebook and filed out with the others. That was another thing she had to thank Mitch for. What in the world had made him come back to San Francisco, anyway? Had he somehow heard how happy she was and decided to see what he could do about it? She could picture him now, lounging in some bar in the Lower East Side, lots of smoke and neon etchings of nudes, when a mutual acquaintance of theirs walked in. What anyone *she* knew might be doing in a place like that she wasn't entirely sure, but she did not stop to rationalize.

"How's Diana?" Mitch would say eventually.

"Great," the friend would reply, his tongue loosened, no doubt by several glasses of very cheap liquor. "Never better, as a matter of fact. Just got a promotion, looks great, feels great, life is perfect...."

"Well," Mitch would declare with a gleam in his eye, "I can fix that."

Whereby he would rise from the table—leaving the friend with the check, of course—and book the first flight to San Francisco.

She was so deep in her brooding thoughts that she didn't hear her name being called. Elise had to leap in front of her, waving a collection of message slips in her face, to get her attention.

Diana blinked and stepped back. "Oh, Elise, I'm sorry. I guess I'm a little distracted. Are those for me?"

"Not exactly, but I thought you'd be interested. While you were...distracted, we've been very busy at the old concierge desk."

Diana took the message slips and began to glance through them, frowning. As per procedure, each slip was logged according to time and room number. The first one was marked 10:35, Oleander Suite. A simple request for toiletries which, according to the check mark at the bottom of the slip, had been immediately fulfilled. There was nothing unusual about that, but Diana's frown deepened with foreboding. She looked at the second slip. 10:43, Oleander Suite. A request for a different brand of shampoo. This was not the kind of whim the concierge desk would normally gratify, but for a suite guest it wasn't unusual to go the extra mile. Again a check mark.

Ten-fifty-two. Could someone run down to Lord & Taylor for him? Silk boxers, size 34. Diana crumpled the note. 11:02. If not Lord & Taylor, how about the local shopping mart? 11:06. Who did they have who could fix a broken zipper? No, a bellman was not what he had in mind. 11:12. A request for bubble bath, granted. The crumbled scraps of paper were beginning to litter the floor around Diana's feet as her lips grew tighter and thinner. 11:18. A request for a masseuse. 11:22. Masseuse canceled, request for someone to wash his back.

Diana balled up the last note, her mouth now a grim line.

"I think he wanted to get your attention," Elise murmured.

"He's got it." It sounded more like a threat than a promise, even to Diana's ears.

"It really wasn't any trouble," Elise said, rather too quickly. "It was kind of fun, in a way. The desk wasn't too busy and—"

"And this has gone far enough." She thrust her notebook into Elise's hands, her face set and her eyes glinting with the light of battle. "Please take my calls. This won't take long."

She turned on her heel and marched toward the elevator, leaving Elise to mutter, "Remind me *never* to get on that woman's bad side."

THE OLEANDER SUITE was on the fifth floor. At either end of the floor, and beside each of the two elevators, were anterooms charmingly arranged to look like parlors. A man was reading a newspaper in the anteroom at the eastern end of the floor, just outside the Oleander Suite. He looked up with a start as Diana, using the passkey she had appropriated from Housekeeping, burst into the suite and slammed the door behind her with a resounding crash. Diana, however, did not even glance at him. She was in a fine, high rage, and nothing could stop her.

She had to admit, however, that she was momentarily at a loss when she stepped into the room and found it deserted.

The Oleander Suite was, appropriately enough, decorated with a painting of oleanders that dominated the wall over the sofa grouping, and the room took its wine, blue and gray color scheme from the painting. The damask upholstery of the sofa had not been disturbed by even the faintest imprint of a body. The wine-colored carpet was spotless. Even the television remained concealed inside its polished cherrywood armoire. A peek inside the bedroom showed a similar lack of disorder. That, Diana observed, was not like Mitch at all. He could wreck a room faster than anyone she had ever known.

Presumably he had been too busy making annoying phone calls since he had checked in to do his customary amount of damage.

She saw his personal items on the desk, so she assumed he hadn't left the suite. Then she heard his voice, muffled by the walls between them, calling sweetly, "Is that you, darling? I'm in here."

Her shoulders squared; her righteous wrath returned. She strode toward the bathroom.

Diana had lived with Mitch long enough to expect almost anything. Had she been in a more rational frame of mind she certainly would have thought twice before bursting unannounced into his bathroom. She was therefore almost relieved when she rounded the corner and saw Mitch sitting in the oversize bathtub, up to his neck in bubbles, watching a game show on the television mounted on the opposite wall and eating what appeared to be a full-course steak dinner.

The room-service cart was drawn up in front of the vanity. On the floor, from the cart to the tub, neatly arranged amidst Mitch's discarded clothing, were trays of other delicacies. Mitch was using the tub tray—a recent innovation designed to allow busy executives to do their paperwork while soaking in the tub—like a

TV tray, cutting into his steak with relish. He greeted Diana with a casual wave of his steak knife.

Diana looked around in a mixture of horror and disbelief. "You're eating in the bathroom," she said flatly.

He glanced around observantly. "Yeah, I guess I am."

"I thought, since meeting you, I had encountered every vile, disgusting, barbaric behavior known to man. But you are *eating in the bathroom.*"

"Naked," he pointed out, slicing off another bite of steak. "I'm eating in the bathroom, naked."

Diana's expression twisted into one of exquisite disdain. "You are the filthiest, most ill-bred man I've ever known."

He raised his fork in mild objection. "Ill-bred, maybe. Filthy..." He indicated the surrounding bubbles. "Hardly." He took a final bite of the steak and pushed the tray along its track to the foot of the tub, sinking into the water with a loud, sloshing wave.

He grinned at her. "So what are you here for, the back scrubbing or the shampoo?"

"You are beneath contempt."

He winked at her. "Just the way you like it, huh, babe?"

Diana's first instinct was to turn and stalk away, but that had too much of a feeling of defeat about it to suit her. She had come here on a mission, and she was not going to leave until it was accomplished.

She stared down at him coolly. "What are you doing here?"

He picked up a bath sponge, dribbling water over his chest. "Isn't it obvious?"

Mitch had always had a nice chest. Diana couldn't help watching now as the little stream of water from the sponge parted the veil of bubbles and glistened over the gentle swell of pectoral muscles, sliding across the slick pattern of dark hair, trickling over the tip of one flat brown nipple. After all this time, she could still remember how his chest felt beneath her hands, slippery with perspiration as her fingers glided across it, defining shape and texture. . . .

She scowled at the direction of her thoughts, and bent to pick up his discarded T-shirt, then his jeans, because she simply couldn't stand looking at them lying crumpled on the floor. Maybe it was habit, maybe it was instinct. She had only been married to Mitch for thirteen months three years ago, but it felt as though she had spent half her adult life picking up his clothes.

"You know perfectly well what I mean," she said sharply, folding the clothes onto the vanity. "What are you doing here, in San Francisco? At the St. Regis?"

"I'm not sure I like your tone, princess. I've come home. Let's have a little rejoicing. Ring the church bells, kill the fatted calf, let the champagne flow—"

"I'll be killing a lot more than a calf if I don't get some answers," Diana warned darkly. "And this is *not* your home."

"You know what they say. Home is the place that, when you go there, they have to take you in."

"Then I suggest you either find another home or a better definition, because I promise you, this hotel does *not* have to take you in. And if you cause any more trouble, you'll find out just exactly what the limits of our hospitality are."

He tilted his head back to look at her with a smile that was calculated to be endearing, soft brown eyes guaranteed to melt the coldest heart.... It was, and it did. "Then how about this?" Mitch asked. "Home is where the heart is."

Diana swallowed hard. *Reason number twenty-seven,* she thought.

For the first few months after the divorce, Diana had spent a great many sleepless nights listing answers to the question, "Why did you marry him, anyway?" Reasons she gave her parents, reasons she gave her co-workers...reasons she gave herself. Reason number twenty-seven: that smile. It made a woman believe that every insincere cliché he spoke was the sheerest poetry composed only for her.

Soon after, of course, Diana had moved on to composing other lists: reasons she *never* should have married him, reasons she should have run the other way the moment she saw him coming.... Those lists were endless.

Fortunately, she had long since outgrown whatever susceptibility to his charm she might once have possessed. It was a simple matter for her now to square her shoulders and reply coolly, "You sound like a chamber of commerce ad."

Mitch abruptly sank below the surface of the water and emerged a second later, shaking his wet hair wildly and flinging water everywhere. Diana gave an exclamation of dismay as she stumbled backward, trying to avoid the shower, and almost stepped on a platter of shrimp.

"You wretched, vulgar—you have the manners of a two-year-old chimpanzee, do you know that?" Diana brushed furiously at her skirt, which, for the second time that day, was water-splotched. "How on earth did you ever escape the zoo?"

"I didn't have to," he replied cheerfully, pouring a measure of shampoo into his palm. "They blew it up around me." He grinned at her as he worked the lather into his hair. "Sure you don't want to help?"

Diana hated herself for it, but she couldn't help noticing the way his lean muscles flexed as he lifted his arms, water oiling his skin . . . noticing, and remembering, and trying very hard to remain objective.

Now, watching him do something as mundane as washing his hair, seeing how the water droplets skated along his bare body, Diana felt a dangerous little prickle of excitement begin far back in her throat.

"What do you mean, they blew it up?" she demanded.

Mitch ducked under the water and surfaced this time as smoothly as a seal, slicking his wet hair back with his fingers. He looked like an old-time gangster.

Diana had no idea how appropriate that comparison was until he replied, "My apartment. They firebombed it."

She stared at him. "Who? The health department?"

He grinned at her, soaping his arms. "That's what I like about you, princess. Always a snappy comeback."

"Well then, who?" Her tone was impatient. "Who's 'they'?"

"You know. They. The bad guys."

"That would seem to me to be a matter of opinion. I always did think I couldn't be the only person in the world who wanted to kill you."

"Maybe you should send them a thank-you note."

"Don't be silly. They missed, didn't they?"

But there was no amusement in Mitch's tone as he replied, "Not by much."

The lighting over the bathtub was soft, and the shadow that fell across Mitch's face made it difficult for Diana to read his expression. But the ghost of a chill went through her with his last words and she said carefully, "I think you're serious."

"Since when have you ever known me to be serious about something as clichéd as life and death? Hell no, that's not serious. What's serious is the bastards blew up my brand-new, state-of-the-art sound system. And I still owed twenty-two hundred dollars on it. That, my dear, is no laughing matter."

Why not? Diana thought, a little dazedly. *Why in the world not?* Wasn't this just Mitch's style? Living on the edge, courting danger, perpetually playing to the crowd.... He wasn't satisfied to merely write cheap melodrama; he had to live it as well. Had there ever been a time in his life that he was not in trouble with *someone?*

"All right," she said very calmly. "We don't seem to be getting anywhere with who. Perhaps you could tell me why."

He lifted one leg out of the water and propped it against the wall, soaping it from ankle to knee. "Beats me, babe. You know yourself I'm the sweetest guy in the world. Never made an enemy in my life. Can't think of anybody who'd want to do me harm."

Deliberately, Diana jerked her eyes away from the shape of his leg. "No? Well, I must say this is a first. No angry bookie breathing down your neck? No determined IRS agent?"

"Those guys," he scoffed. "No sense of humor whatsoever."

"No bitter girlfriend, no jealous ex-husband—"

He cut her off with a penetrating look. "I really don't think it's your place to speculate about my personal life, do you, princess? Not anymore."

She felt a flush of shame warm the back of her neck and she knew he was right. She hated it when he did that. Mitch DeSalvo, who could give lessons in dirty fighting, who had the morals of an alley cat, dared to tell her what she could and couldn't do—and he was right. Even worse, he could, with a single look, a quiet word, make her feel like a child who had just spilled ink on her penmanship paper. *Damn him,* she thought. *What am I doing here, anyway? Why do I keep letting him do this to me?*

And yet she stayed, her fists closing and her lips tightening, and waited for an explanation.

He turned his attention to the other leg. "Do you know my book, *City Heat?*"

Diana replied coolly, "I do not."

But of course she knew it. Mitch, under a dozen or so pseudonyms, made an obscene amount of money churning out the kind of slick paperback detective novels that Diana was embarrassed to pick up in the drugstore but which the general public seemed to find enormously appealing. One of the pseudonyms, Sal Mitchell, seemed to be particularly popular, and to Diana's annoyance it was becoming more and more difficult *not* to hear about the latest Sal Mitchell release.

"Well," Mitch said, splashing water over his shoulders and chest, "the truth is, *City Heat* isn't entirely a work of fiction, despite what the disclaimer in the front of the book says. And it seems certain people aren't very happy about having their secrets told in print."

He lifted himself out of the tub and stood before her for a moment, naked and completely unselfconscious, or perhaps deliberately provocative. Diana couldn't tell and didn't care, because for just a moment the sight of his body, so familiar, once so adored, brought back memories and sensations that blotted out everything else. The way the mat of hair on his chest tapered into a V below his waist and thickened again low on his abdomen, cupping his sex. The tan lines that began midthigh, demonstrating his preference for cutoff denims instead of a traditional swimsuit. The flat muscles of his thighs, the shape of his buttocks and his ankles and even his toes.... A collage of impressions—tastes, scents, textures—bombarded her senses. This time she didn't even ask why. She knew.

Mitch reached casually for a towel, and the motion jarred Diana back to the present. She said, through a throat that was quite a bit drier than it had been a moment ago, "What kind of people?"

He wrapped the towel around his waist and looped another behind his neck, drying his back and shoulders. "The kind of people that blow up apartments, unfortunately."

Comprehension slowly dawned, leaving Diana cold. "Do you mean—criminals?"

"Well, yes. In my opinion anybody who tries to blow me up is a criminal."

He moved before the mirror, towel drying his hair, and Diana stared at him. It was a moment before she could make her voice work.

"Do you mean *that's* why you left New York? Because criminals were chasing you?"

He tossed the towel aside and scooped up a handful of shrimp, popping them into his mouth one by one as he used his fingers to comb back his tousled hair. "I left New York," he pointed out, "because my apartment was a pile of cinders. I didn't have a bed to sleep in. I didn't have a refrigerator to eat out of. I didn't even have a change of underwear." He frowned into the mirror. "Still don't, as a matter of fact."

"But why come here?" Diana cried. "Why not go to Florida—that's where your parents are! Or to Chicago, where your brother lives, or—"

He gave her an astonished look in the mirror. "Come on, princess, what kind of guy do you think I am? These people mean business. Do you think I'm going to bring that kind of trouble to my family?"

"But you have no problem at all bringing that kind of trouble to *me!*"

He turned and winked and pinched her cheek. "Heaven help the bad guys if they tangle with you, babe. Why do you think I came here, anyway? I needed somebody big and strong to take care of me."

She jerked angrily away from his touch. "That's just typical of you, isn't it? Why should I even be surprised? You've brought me nothing but trouble since the day I met you. You *specialize* in causing me trouble! You lie awake nights thinking of new and inventive ways to—"

She did not know why she didn't see it coming. She *should* have seen it coming. They were standing less than a foot apart; she could feel the steamy heat from his body and see the mahogany-colored flecks in his eyes. Her fists were clenched and her face was hot with angry color and her voice was rising, when suddenly his hands closed on either side of her face and his mouth covered hers.

It was not a kiss; it was an invasion. Heat and power and taste went through her like a shock wave, overloading her nerves and branding every part of her with the sheer, raw essence of him. His tongue did not explore her mouth; it claimed it, thrusting inside her as though it were his right to do so, filling her with the hot slippery taste of him, taking away her breath, weakening the muscles of her stomach, making colors explode inside her head. She hated him because he could still do that to her and she hated herself for letting him. But she did not try to break away. She didn't want to.

His knee pushed between her thighs as much as her slim skirt would allow, a slow, sensuous movement rubbing the silk lining of her skirt against the inside of her leg just where her stocking ended. Dimly she was aware that the towel around his waist had fallen away and she could feel him, hard and naked against her. She could feel him, she could inhale him, she was infused by him. It had always been like that between them, fireworks and summer storms, earthquakes and thunder and roaring volcanic eruptions. It hadn't changed. She must have known from the beginning that it never would.

Reason number eleven, she thought dazedly, and then slowly, thoroughly, he brought the kiss to an end. He looked down at her.

There was a flush on the surface of his skin, and Diana could feel the heat in her own face, as well. His heat, her heat, lips that were swollen and muscles that were quivering and the taste of him inside her, everywhere.... But the gleam in his eyes was smug and deliberate, and he touched her lips with a light reproving gesture.

"There, you see," he said. "I do know how to do a few things besides cause you trouble."

Diana stiffened. "That's your solution to everything, isn't it? One of your magic kisses and everything is all right."

He dropped his hands to her shoulders. "I've never known it to hurt."

Diana shrugged off his touch, taking a step backward. "Well, guess what?" She kept her voice cold and her smile cool. "It doesn't work anymore. The master must be losing his touch because your kisses don't do anything for me. I am completely unaffected."

"Yeah, I know what you mean." That wicked, far-too-satisfied twinkle in his eyes did not fade, and he glanced down at his naked body deliberately. "Me, too."

With great effort Diana kept her eyes on his face and her voice even. "You," she said, "are a pig."

"So I've been told."

Her fists tightened. "I hate you."

"I know."

"I hope they find you and blow you to bits."

"I know."

"But," she said tightly, and whirled on her heel, "they'd better not do it in *my* hotel!"

Mitch waited until the entrance door slammed behind her—hard enough to shake the light fixture over the bathroom mirror—then he let the grin slide over his features. There were few things in this world that gave him quite as much satisfaction as knowing he had been the cause of one of Diana's world-class door slams.

He gave himself a congratulatory thumbs-up in the mirror, then turned to dress. When he left the suite a few minutes later, he was whistling.

The man on the divan outside the Oleander Suite waited until Mitch reached the elevators and punched the button for the lobby. Then he rose, quietly folded his newspaper and followed him.

Chapter Three

Mitch loved San Francisco. He loved the fact that, within a one-block radius of the high-priced St. Regis Hotel, he could step over a drunk, buy a diamond bracelet in a place that provided a security escort back to his hotel, or have lunch in a tearoom so exclusive that even those with a Nob Hill zip code had to wait three months for a table. And he loved the fact that he could walk into the St. Regis carrying a brown paper bag—a bag that might contain anything from a bottle of Wild Turkey Bourbon to a bomb—and receive only the warmest of greetings from the doorman. He, who twenty years ago wouldn't have been able to walk into a place like the St. Regis at all.

Actually, the bag contained nothing more exciting than a couple of T-shirts. He left it at the desk with a five-dollar bill and a request that it be sent up to his room. The remainder of his purchases were already en route. He turned for the bar.

Diana was not at the concierge desk. He did not stop at her office. He did not, in fact, even look in that direction.

The Zephyr Room was one of those dark, stately bars that catered to the executive with three half-million-dollar deals in the works, where a man could toss down a couple of Scotch-and-waters for not much less than the price of a bottle of Chivas, and where the stereo played Bach. Tourists never came there. Ladies never popped in for a luncheon Dubonnet. And those were basically the only two things the Zephyr Room had to recommend it.

Mitch pulled open the heavy glass-and-oak door and politely stepped back, gesturing for the man behind him to precede. The man took a corner table and opened his newspaper. Mitch sat at the bar and ordered a shot and a beer, which he figured even a place like the Zephyr Room couldn't wreck too badly.

At two o'clock in the afternoon the bar was almost empty. In another two hours it would start to fill up, for the Zephyr Room was exactly the kind of place at which cultural snobs liked to gather before and after a major social event. Mitch used to like to hang out there and just eavesdrop: *But my dear, being at the top of the social register in Seattle is a distinction roughly the equivalent of being the finest cellist in all of Lubbock. I mean, really. How much competition can there be?* And, *Of course I told him that his choice of life-*

style was entirely up to him—what else can an enlightened parent do?—but I absolutely refused to pay for a wedding in Golden Gate Park, particularly to a man I barely knew! He used to memorize some of the best ones and repeat them later to Diana just to annoy her. Sometimes he was rewarded by seeing her lips twitch with a repressed smile. Of course, toward the end, the smiles had become fewer and farther between, and so had Mitch's efforts to elicit them.

Sometimes he still wondered how things between them had ever managed to go so bad so quickly.... And then he'd have to remind himself that things between them had never been all that great in the first place. They had, in fact, been impossible. Never in his life had he known a woman so sure of herself, so demanding, so unyielding, so completely wrong for him . . . and so impossible to resist.

If she had been wearing a sign that said *Danger, Nuclear Reactor,* the warning couldn't have been more clear—and he couldn't have run any faster into her arms. Because that was what it was like, being with her: nuclear meltdown, fifteen megaton explosion, completely out of control. Small stars went supernova with less force than the two of them generated when they were together. Planets imploded, worlds collided, whole civilizations went up in smoke . . . that was what it was like when they were together. Was it any wonder that, with that kind of destructive energy ricocheting through the atmosphere, his brain had gotten a little fried? Just enough to make him believe that marrying her was the only sensible thing to do. Just enough to make him think he couldn't live without her, not for another hour, another minute....

Just enough to make him keep coming back here, even now, when he was old enough and smart enough to know better. Damn it, after all this time, he *knew* better.

The bartender brought his shot and beer. He was a young blond man whose uniform was a tuxedo shirt, tie and cummerbund. Mitch did not know him. There had been a time when he knew every bartender in this city by name.

Mitch downed the shot and chased it with a couple of long swallows of beer. One thing he had to say for the St. Regis: they never forgot to frost the mugs.

"Been working here long?" Mitch asked.

The bartender picked up a cloth and started polishing the glasses. "Almost a year."

Mitch gave a short shake of his head. "Jeez, have I been away that long?"

He stuck out his hand. "The name's Mitch. If this trip is anything like the others, we'll be seeing a lot of each other."

The bartender grinned and shook his hand. "I'm Jon. Do you live in the city, then? You said you'd been away."

Mitch took another swallow of beer. "Used to. I was born here, as a matter of fact. North Beach."

"No kidding? Man, that's a place that's changed."

"Not really. It always was an exciting piece of the city. Now it's just better to enjoy the excitement with a weapon in your pocket."

Jon chuckled. "So what brings you back? You got family here?"

"God, no. I transplanted them a long time ago. That took some doing, let me tell you. Did you ever try to move an Italian mother *and* grandmother from the house they've lived in for forty years? They wouldn't trust the movers with the important stuff, and my pop couldn't see well enough to drive. So it was just me, them, a cat, a canary and twenty-five cartons of their most prized possessions, driving from California to Florida...man, it was like *Grapes of Wrath.*" He drained his beer. "It was at that moment I decided to stay single."

He dropped his eyes to his empty mug and muttered, almost against his will, "I'd be a happy man today if I'd only stuck with that decision."

Then he took a pack of cigarettes from his pocket and shook one out. "Hey, this is too hackneyed even for me. Bartenders really don't spend their time listening to other people's troubles, and believe me, I've known enough bartenders to qualify as an expert. You've got things to do."

"Not really. That's why I like this shift. The tips aren't great, but it gives me plenty of time to study."

Jon produced a lighter from his pocket but Mitch shook his head, sticking the unlit cigarette in his mouth. "So what are you studying?"

Jon reached beneath the bar and pulled out a book, setting it in front of Mitch. The title was *Human Sexuality*.

Mitch shook his head. "Times sure have changed since I went to school."

Jon grinned. "I'm a medical student. Second year."

Mitch nodded, tapping the cigarette against the bar in an absent fashion. "So." He indicated the book. "Did you find the answer yet?"

"To what?"

"The Question." He paused. "What Do Women Want?"

Jon chuckled. "Easy. The same thing we want, only better."

Mitch lifted his mug to him. "To youth and innocence. May you lose neither before your time." He drained the last of the beer. "Set me up again, Jon, and I'll leave you alone. You've obviously got a lot of studying to do."

"Actually, I'm off duty in a couple of minutes. I'm working a party tonight and I've got to get home and get a little shut-eye."

"Moonlighting, huh?"

"Not really. The party's in the Crown Ballroom, and Miss Moore tries to give the guys on staff first shot at extra work like that."

Mitch's attention sharpened. "Moore? You mean the concierge lady? What's she got to do with it?"

Jon's brows knit briefly. "I'm not sure, really. Some bigwig Texan has flown in to give an engagement party for his daughter. All kinds of society types are going to be there, foreign dignitaries, you know. Miss Moore usually has a hand in something that fancy. Should be quite a bash."

"Do you think she'll be there?" Mitch asked casually.

"At the party?" He shrugged. "Probably. I think she's a friend of the family. Anyway, it pays a hundred dollars just for showing up, and you wouldn't believe the kind of tips these Texans let go of once they've got a few glasses of champagne inside them."

"Yeah, I bet," Mitch murmured. Then he smiled, flipped the soggy cigarette into a nearby ashtray and laid a couple of bills on the bar. "See you later, Jon. I've got some phone calls to make." He took the mug of beer with him as he started for the door, calling over his shoulder, "And thanks! You've been a big help."

FOR THE REST of the day Diana managed not to think about Mitch—or at least not to see him. Thinking about Mitch was like a disease; she couldn't just cure it by force of will. She therefore kept herself busy with the myriad details of her job. She managed not to think about him more than a couple of dozen times during the remainder of the day.

It was not part of her function as director of guest relations to plan affairs on the scale of the Holston engagement party. But because her father was acquainted with Jason Holston, and because the Holstons had been gracious enough to send her an invitation to the party, Diana took a particular interest in seeing that everything went as smoothly as possible.

The Crown Ballroom was, in keeping with the rest of the hotel, small but elegant.

When Diana checked the room at four-thirty, the tables were already set up and swathed with festoons of pink satin, decorated with centerpieces of sweetheart roses. The walls were similarly draped in various shades of rose, and enormous baskets of flowers were being set up in every available space.

"Yuck." Elise, walking beside her, wrinkled her nose and shuddered elaborately. "I feel like I'm inside a giant intestine."

Diana smiled absently. "It's not so bad." She peeked inside an open carton and discovered the etched crystal stemware that was to be used as party favors. She raised her voice a little and signaled to one of the boys who was setting up. "Excuse me. You won't forget that these champagne glasses are supposed to have pink ribbons tied around the stems, will you?''

Elise groaned. "I'm going to gag in a minute. Why are you doing this, anyway? Are they paying you extra?"

"Good heavens, no! It's just that the Holstons are family friends and I want everything to be nice."

"Exactly. With friends that rich, what are you doing checking other people's stemware and arranging other people's flowers? I mean, doesn't it make you feel funny, hobnobbing with the hoi polloi by night after spending the day in the salt mines with the rest of us minimum-wage earners?"

Diana mentally counted the number of roses in three randomly selected centerpieces. It was not unusual for florists to cheat on a rose here and there to cut costs. "I never thought about it," she replied to Elise's question, and nodded with approval when the centerpieces all came out with the right number of roses.

"That," murmured Elise with a baffled shake of her head, "is real class."

Diana glanced up from the notation she was making on her clipboard. "Hmm?"

Elise just laughed. "Never mind. Say, speaking of class, did you get the message from Etienne?"

Diana stared at her.

"I left it on your desk."

"I haven't been in my office all afternoon."

"Well, it's all right. He didn't want you to call back or anything. He just said he'd pick you up at home at seven-thirty if it was all right."

"I was supposed to call and confirm the party with him today. I can't believe I forgot."

"I can't believe you forgot someone as gorgeous as Etienne, either! You're not looking to trade him in for a newer model are you?"

"I *never* forget. I can't imagine what's wrong with me." But her lips tightened with impatience. She knew exactly what was wrong with her. Mitch DeSalvo.

She hadn't thought of Etienne once all day. Perhaps the gentlest, most romantic, interesting, handsome, far-too-good-to-be-true man she had ever met . . . and he just slipped her mind. She would be attending this very party with him in less than three hours and she had simply overlooked it. Who else could possibly be responsible for that kind of mental deterioration except Mitch DeSalvo?

Suddenly there was a rumbling sensation beneath their feet; glasses rattled and tables shuddered briefly. A few of the boys stopped working to watch the big chandelier sway overhead. Most of them didn't even look up. Elise groaned softly and clutched Diana's arm as the tremor subsided.

"I *hate* it when that happens," she said sincerely.

Diana laughed, her attention effectively diverted from its previous dark ruminations. "I guess you know you've been here too long when you don't even notice anymore."

"Oh, come on. It doesn't bother you, even a little bit?"

"Not really." Diana made another notation on the clipboard, and added, "I've got enough phobias and neuroses without worrying about earthquakes."

"You?" Elise eyed her skeptically. "Strong men cower when they hear your footsteps in the hall. Small children scurry for cover at the sound of your voice. Let me tell you, honey, I don't want to meet up with whatever it is that scares you." Then she insisted curiously, "So what is it?"

Diana fought with a grin. "Come on, I've got to get back to the office."

"Now I've *got* to know."

"I'm going to leave a note for the evening shift that if the Holstons have any problems before the party, they can call me at home. Will you make sure Evan gets it?"

"Di—an-a." Elise drew out her name in a way that was meant to be intimidating, and painted a severe expression on her face. It was impossible for a face as beautiful as hers to ever look stern, however, so the effect was somewhat less than she had intended.

"Are you going to take a chance on alienating the only person at this hotel who was ever nice to you just because she *liked* you?" demanded Elise. "Do you want to risk my never telling you another deep, dark, intimate personal secret?"

Diana looked at her, surprised. "You've never told me any intimate secrets."

"Well, I might. Someday. Come on," she urged. "Tell. What are you afraid of?"

Diana started walking again. "Lots of things."

"Like what?"

"I slept with a night-light until I was twelve."

"Everybody does that. That's nothing."

"Heights. I'm terrified of heights."

"That must be what kept you out of the air force."

"I'm serious. Ever since I was a child. In gym class they used to laugh at me on the rope climb. I'd get halfway up and then freeze. Same thing with the high dive."

"Well," conceded Elise, somewhat reluctantly, "I suppose that's something. Of course, it's not much consolation to all those people—from the mechanic who services your Mercedes to the manager of this very hotel—who are afraid of *you*."

Diana tore off the note for the night shift and flipped closed the cover of her clipboard. "Well, there's not much I can do about that, is there? Good heavens, that reminds me—I forgot to call someone to fix my tire. It's a good thing Etienne is calling for me, or I'd have to take a taxi tonight.''

Elise went on in that same casual, conversational tone, ''Of course, if you ask me, there's only one thing in this world you're really afraid of.'' She slid a sly glance toward Diana as they reached the concierge desk. ''And he happens to be occupying the Oleander Suite right now.''

Expressionlessly, Diana looked at Elise for a moment. Then she handed Elise the note and said, ''Make sure that Evan gets this before you leave, please. I'll see you in the morning.''

THE RAIN HAD STOPPED, but the fog that sagged over the city in its place was the perfect match for Diana's mood as she made her way home that afternoon. The city was colorless, damp and chill, and all she really wanted to do was curl up in the warm paneled study in front of a glowing fire with a bottle of Montrechet and an enormous bowl of ice cream.

Afraid of Mitch, indeed. Diana Elizabeth Moore, of the Boston Moores and Nantucket Havershams, had been raised to fear no man, least of all a cocky, ill-bred, tin-plated slob like Mitch DeSalvo. She was annoyed with him, plagued by him, exasperated by him, very often pushed to the point of desperation by him, but she was not afraid of him. She was afraid of what he could do to her peace of mind every time he showed up here.

He was an albatross around her neck, the bad penny that kept turning up, proof positive that some mistakes couldn't be rectified no matter how hard one tried. And now that Elise had brought the subject up, nothing Diana could do would put him out of her mind.

Another foggy evening, another San Francisco street. The echo of footsteps behind her, matching her pace, making her heart beat faster and stronger with alarm. She walked faster. So did her stalker. She turned a corner, onto a narrow, unfamiliar street. The footsteps followed. She climbed a set of sidewalk steps, emerging onto another unfamiliar street. The footsteps were closer now. She turned again and suddenly the footsteps outmatched her, running. Diana stood perfectly still and awaited her fate.

Mitchell DeSalvo appeared beside her in the fog, grinning, breathing a little harder than normal with exertion. "Lost, Miss Moore?"

Diana scowled at the memory as the cable car came to a stop at the bottom of her street. For the last time that day she jostled her way through the crowd of tourists and commuters and disembarked. She began the steep climb up the foggy street toward home.

I assure you, Mr. DeSalvo, I am not lost.

The voices from that long-ago day drifted back to her like ghosts through the fog. Diana knew from experience the futility of trying to silence them. Once he took hold, Mitch was inexorcisable; fighting him was a waste of energy—as she had learned on that foggy night almost four years ago.

"A long way from home, then."

He fell into step beside her cheerfully, with an easy rolling gait that exuded confidence and a kind of jungle grace. He moved like a cat through the fog. Diana's heart was still pounding, but it had nothing to do with her previous alarm.

"You can't possibly have any idea where home is for me. And before I call for the police, I'd very much like to hear your explanation for why you were following me."

He chuckled softly. "You can call till your voice gives out in this part of town. Nobody pays attention unless you're gushing blood from one or more severed limbs."

"I have lived in San Francisco for four years and I repeat—"

"You're not lost, I know. Just temporarily misplaced, then. Maybe just misplaced enough to need a bodyguard?"

"Don't be absurd! I wouldn't even be lost if you hadn't been chasing me—"

He burst into laughter. *"I do like a stubborn woman!"*

Diana's heels clicked more rapidly on the damp pavement and she scowled, but inside her chest, sunshine was bursting and she couldn't even begin to explain why. "It is a matter of supreme indifference to me, Mr. DeSalvo, what you like."

"Take those steps and you'll be headed back toward Nob Hill."

"That was not where I was headed."

"Could've fooled me."

"Something tells me that's not at all difficult to do."

He chuckled again and the sound was like a caress, reaching out to her in the fog. Diana found herself smiling secretly and was glad he couldn't see.

She took the steps because, even though Nob Hill was not her destination, it was at least familiar. He stayed beside her.

"You have yet to explain why you were following me, Mr. DeSalvo."

Again the voice that caressed, rather than simply speaking the words. The voice that could send chills up her spine and make her skin glow with an inexplicable heat. The voice that made her knees weak as he said softly, "I think you know why, Miss Moore."

She stopped. He was very close.

"Tell me."

He kissed her, and all the world changed.

Diana's house came into view, an elegant confection of pale yellow and white, three stories of gracious curves and stately angles. Mitch had wanted an Italianate facade in garish colors of purple and rose. They had argued about that extensively. Not that there was ever a doubt as to whose opinion would prevail and not that Mitch had ever really cared about the matter. Things that represented permanence and commitment were not within Mitch DeSalvo's scope of interest, and arguing had always been more of a habit between them than a method of communication.

Diana loved the house more than anything she had ever owned, and usually the mere sight of it was enough to chase away her bleakest mood. Today, however, it only reminded her of Mitch.

There was no escaping him, she thought sourly as she turned the key. The only thing to do was try to ignore him.

Unfortunately, that was a great deal easier said than done.

Chapter Four

Diana had been conditioned throughout her life never to get too attached to anything. It was a philosophy that had worked just fine until she saw The House.

The House had survived the Great Fire of 1906 and the earthquake of 1989. It had survived the marriage of Diana Moore to Mitch DeSalvo. It was for Diana a symbol of all that was permanent, lasting and indestructible in life. It was the home she had always wanted and, for a brief time with Mitch, had almost had. It was Mitch's wedding gift to her, and perhaps the only good thing that had ever come of their meeting.

The foyer was narrow with an uneven brick floor, but it was three stories high, lit from the top by an octagonal stained-glass window planted square in the middle of the ceiling. Diana loved it because it was unique. It gave the house character.

There were other architectural surprises—character lines, Diana liked to call them—that weren't nearly as pleasant. Like the wrought-iron spiral staircase that dominated the tiny foyer. Mitch had hated that staircase. They spent one whole weekend painting it white, hoping to make it appear lighter and more attractive, but all they had succeeded in doing was making it white. At the end of the job they'd stood in overalls and painters' caps, tired and disgruntled as they surveyed their handiwork. Mitch had said something that made her laugh. They had ended up making love there in the tiny foyer. The afternoon light through the stained glass had danced across their skin in translucent fantasy colors.

On the entry level was the beautifully paneled library. Diana had furnished it with cast-off antiques from her parents' city house, which added that touch of tradition that was so important to her. That was her favorite room in the house, and the only room that was completely finished.

There was a formal dining room, a small office and a spacious kitchen, which the designer Diana had hired—and Mitch promptly fired—had wanted to turn into a black-and-white gourmet showcase.

The second story was dominated by a huge circular master bedroom and open bath with a claw-footed tub. Mitch, with his customary barroom taste, had wanted to furnish the bedroom with a round bed and mirrored ceiling. Diana had assured him that if he did so, he would be sleeping alone. They had compromised with a king-size four-poster in heavy mahogany.

When Mitch moved out, Diana had gone on a vengeful decorating spree, draping the bed in yards of net canopy, ordering a sprigged rose coverlet, draping the windows in coordinating stripes and flowers. It was a Victorian confection taken to the perfect extreme, and Mitch would have hated every inch of it.

That was Diana's second favorite room of the house.

Usually her house was her haven; she could close the door and leave whatever miseries plagued the day outside. But tonight her nerves were coiled tight, and not even the warmth of every lamp in the house could dispel her uneasiness. There was a tight, anxious feeling in her stomach, and she knew from experience that would be the state of her nerves until Mitch DeSalvo finally skulked back to whatever corner of the swamp he had crawled out of. The trouble with Mitch, of course, was that she couldn't just close the door and leave him outside—of her house, of her thoughts, of her life.

But for one evening, at least, she was going to *try* to keep him at the very back of her mind. An elegant party, surrounded by people of refinement and taste, aged wine, fine music, Etienne . . . an evening like that was the only remedy for a day like the one she'd had. She only wished the party was not being held at the hotel. There was far too much chance of meeting Mitch in the hall.

The fog had delayed her, so Diana didn't have time for the long soak in the tub she had promised herself. She took a quick shower instead and chose from her wardrobe an ivory sheath with an ivory and silver-shot jacket that draped like gossamer and felt like angels' wings against her skin. The dress had cost her a month's salary, but it was worth every penny.

She fashioned her hair into a lover's knot, low on her neck and accented by a large ivory bow. Her only other ornamentation was a small diamond heart pendant that her father had given her for her sixteenth birthday, and a pair of matching earrings her mother had given her for her twenty-first.

Etienne rang the doorbell at five minutes to seven. He was, Diana thought as she greeted him, quite possibly the most stunning man ever to wear a tuxedo. He had the kind of elegant, old-world beauty that was perfectly suited to formal wear: dark, lively eyes, rich brown curly hair, a slightly olive complexion with the faintest hint of a beard shadow even when he was closely shaven....

With a start, Diana realized that description could have applied to Mitch. Etienne was *nothing* like Mitch. Where Mitch was tight and compact, Etienne was slender, almost willowy. Etienne's features were long and aristocratic; Mitch's were square and blunt. And Etienne's manners were . . . well, there was simply no comparison. Diana could not even recall using the word manners in the same sentence with Mitch's name, unless it was to comment on his lack of them.

Etienne took her hands and kissed her cheek lightly. "Diana," he said warmly. "You are a goddess, as always."

"You have little flecks of mahogany in your eyes," Diana said, without meaning to. "I never noticed that before."

He laughed, squeezing her hands, and the light caught the flecks in his eyes and made them dance. "My darling, do you see why I adore you? Always, you surprise me!"

Diana's smile was a little absent as he tucked her arm through his and escorted her to the car. So she liked men with dark hair and eyes; a lot of women did. It meant nothing. But why had she never noticed the similarity between Etienne's looks and Mitch's before? And why in the world was she letting it bother her so?

Diana had met Etienne when he was the chargé d'affaires for the French ambassador. He was now attached to the French consulate in San Francisco. Their relationship already was beginning to show a great deal of promise and provided each of them with a well-dressed, charming, and cultured companion for occasions such as the Holstons' engagement party.

We are a fine looking couple, she observed with satisfaction when she caught a glimpse of their reflection in the revolving door of the St. Regis lobby. And by that time she had completely forgotten to make comparisons to Mitch.

"How tiring it must be for you to return to your work for your recreation," remarked Etienne as they made their way toward the ballroom. "It is—*comment dit-on?*—a cobbler's vacation?"

Diana laughed and slapped at his arm playfully with her evening purse. "Busman's holiday!" she provided, though she suspected Etienne knew the correct expression perfectly well. He simply liked to make her laugh.

"Ah, yes," he acceded soberly. "And what is your expression about the cobbler?"

"Do you mean his children having no shoes?"

"Not appropriate, I would think." They reached the doorway of the ballroom, and he presented their invitations.

"I'm forced to agree." Diana smiled at the liveried attendant who took their invitations. "Good evening, Marshall. Is everything going well?"

"Good evening, Miss Moore. No problem that I know about."

"There, you see." With an arm gently around her shoulders Etienne ushered her away. "You are a guest and still you are working. Busman's holiday."

"Well, it is part of my job. Besides, I—" Then she saw him, and the words dried up in her throat.

Mitch DeSalvo was leaning against one of the rose-and-ribbon wrapped columns, watching her with one of his small secret smiles. When she noticed him, he lifted his glass in salute, then ambled toward them.

He was wearing a champagne-colored jacket of raw silk over jeans and a T-shirt that proclaimed "The Best Things in Life are Italian or Chocolate." Amidst the glittering, black-tie-and-diamond crowd, he was as out of place as a tiger in a ballroom and, naturally, the focus of attention of everyone in the room. Curious feminine smiles slanted in his direction. Gentlemen, too polite to interrupt their conversations to stare, followed him with their eyes over the glasses of champagne. It was a role Mitch not only enjoyed, it had practically been invented for him.

"Why, princess," he drawled as he reached them. "Fancy meeting you here."

Diana was too outraged—too utterly shocked and disappointed and angry with whatever fate had brought him here—to speak. *One evening,* she thought. *One evening was all I asked....*

Etienne, upon whose mastery of awkward social situations international peace could at times depend, smiled politely. "Darling, do you know this gentleman?"

Mitch just returned his smile, and Diana managed shortly, "Yes. He's my husband."

Etienne lifted an eyebrow. "My, my. You *are* an interesting woman."

"*Ex*-husband," Diana corrected tightly. "My ex-husband. Mitch DeSalvo. Mitch, this is Etienne Randolais."

"Ah, yes." Etienne extended his hand. "Diana has spoken often of you. You have excellent taste in restored Victorian homes."

"Also in women," agreed Mitch, shaking his hand.

Etienne's pleasant expression did not waver. "Indeed."

Diana, however, lacked Etienne's patience. "What are you doing here, Mitch?" she demanded flatly.

"Sweetie, this is my town." He tapped out a cigarette and waved the hand that held the package around the room. "You don't really think a big society event like this could go down without me, do you?"

"Who," she insisted, keeping her voice even with an effort, "did you bribe for an invitation?"

He grinned. "Hobart Freeman. The society reporter with the *Chronicle?*"

"I know who he is," snapped Diana. "I might have known he'd be low enough—"

"Darling," Etienne interjected smoothly, touching her arm. "Perhaps we should greet our hosts now."

Diana drew in a short breath, feeling as gauche and lacking in manners as Mitch was—and furious with him for bringing her down to his level. After a moment she brought her temper under control and said, "Of course." She inclined her head coolly to Mitch. "Excuse us."

"You bet."

"He is not at all what I expected," murmured Etienne.

Diana resisted the urge to look over her shoulder at Mitch as she muttered in reply, "He never is."

THE EVENING WAS RUINED, of course. It was a peculiar talent of Mitch's, the ability to turn what should have been one of the most pleasant occasions of Diana's life into the most disastrous—all the while having a perfectly marvelous time himself, of course. And that was without a doubt what irked Diana the most. The Holstons adored him. Alyssa Holston's fiancé, Gregory Nelson-Barre, was completely taken in by him, as were all of the Nelson-Barres, the Colters, the Vernons, and everyone else with whom he made contact.

The worst part was that word had somehow begun to circulate that Diana was responsible for his presence here. Thankfully, few had managed to piece together the truth about her relationship with him, possibly because Mitch had not told the same story twice about who he was. She endured the squeezes of the arm, the pats on the hand and the awed hushed whispers with a stoic smile: "Darling, he's simply marvelous! Where on earth did you find him?" "A jungle explorer, just imagine!" "I had no idea the space program was recruiting herbalists. Fascinating chap, just fascinating." "Of course, I've been a great fan of his music for simply ages. He really is something of a cult hero, you know."

Diana smiled and nodded and murmured semi-appropriate responses. She kept herself calm by imagining all the ways a man might be made to suffer before finally gasping his last at the hands of a woman who had finally, irretrievably, been pushed too far.

She swallowed expensive champagne as though it were medicine. She danced obligatory dances with her hosts, selected dignitaries and Etienne, making certain to desert the floor the moment she saw Mitch coming. And she had a thoroughly horrid time. At last she sought shelter at one of the smaller tables with Etienne and a plate of hors d'oeuvres, glassy eyed with exhaustion and too tired even to try to escape when she saw Mitch bearing down on them.

Etienne raised his glass to her with a twinkle in his eyes. "To grace under pressure," he said.

"Death to the oppressor," Diana replied darkly, raising her own glass.

Mitch pulled out a chair and made himself comfortable. "Well, kids," he greeted them expansively. "Having a good time?"

"Not, apparently, as much as you are." To Diana's annoyance, Etienne's amusement appeared to be genuine. "I can't recall the last time any one guest ever caused quite so much excitement at one of these functions, can you, Diana?"

"No." Diana lifted a stuffed mushroom. "But then, so few of us have ever had the opportunity to attend a party with Bonzo the Clown."

"Of course," Mitch said, ignoring her, "to keep from spoiling the effect, I'll have to disappear on the stroke of midnight."

"Leaving them all wondering 'who was that masked man?'" Etienne suggested.

Mitch grinned and shook out a cigarette. "Something like that."

"It's almost eleven now," Diana pointed out.

"Might one ask why you don't simply use your genuine identity, which I'm quite certain would be just as impressive to those in attendance as any assumed persona?" Etienne picked up the pink souvenir matchbook that lay near his place setting and offered it to Mitch. Mitch waved it away, removing the cigarette from his mouth.

"Not nearly as much fun," he answered. "Besides, I'm undercover."

"I see." Etienne glanced at Diana with another twinkle of amusement, inviting her to join the game.

But Diana had long since ceased to find anything about Mitch DeSalvo amusing, and she said abruptly, "Excuse me. I need more champagne."

She started to rise, but Etienne waved her down. "I'll get a waiter, darling. I should mingle, anyway. Stay and enjoy yourself. You've hardly had a moment to sit down all evening."

Diana widened her eyes at him expressively, but apparently not understanding her message, he stood and excused himself.

When he was gone Diana scowled at her empty glass. "I don't know why he did that. He knows I can't stand you."

Mitch chuckled, lifted his hand, and in only a matter of seconds a waiter appeared with two glasses of champagne. Diana frowned but did not refuse the glass when he offered it to her. Mitch didn't mind; he sometimes thought her frowns were more attractive than her smiles—or perhaps it was simply that he had seen them more often.

"I like your boyfriend," he said.

Diana gave him a withering look and sipped her champagne. She did withering looks better than anyone Mitch had ever known.

"No kidding," he insisted. "I think he's cute as hell. I'd take him home myself if I weren't already so crazy about you."

She shifted her gaze away in the perfect pretense of boredom. "You just couldn't pass up the chance, could you?"

"The chance to what?"

"Ruin yet another evening for me."

He made a deprecating gesture with the hand that held the unlit cigarette. "You've had so many evenings. I didn't figure you'd begrudge me just one."

"You figured wrong." She raked him with a cool glance. "The least you could've done is dressed."

He feigned surprise. "I am dressed. And rather well, I thought."

"This is a formal affair."

"And I'm an eccentric, an *artiste*. I'm expected to look like this. You wouldn't want me to disappoint my public, would you?"

"Your public," Diana pointed out without blinking an eye, "tried to assassinate you."

Mitch lifted his glass to her, grinning. "Touché, baby."

Diana, he thought, looked magnificent. She had a great figure—softly rounded breasts, smooth waist, slender hips—and she wasn't afraid to show it off. Her skinny little dress did that to perfection. The square neck skimmed over the top of her breasts, so that a man had to strain to get even a glimpse of cleavage, which of course made what he could see all that much more exciting. Her skirt stopped several inches above her knees, and she had incredible knees—smooth, delicate, the essence of femininity. The ivory-colored jacket was the same length as the dress beneath it, and its shifting, curve-caressing folds hung as artfully as the drapery on a Grecian statue. Mitch knew from looking at it that the material would be lingerie soft, and that touching it, feeling the smooth curves and silky heat of the flesh beneath it, would make him feel as though he were tasting heaven.

Diana looked uncomfortable. "Stop doing that."

"What?"

"Looking at me as though you were planning to have me for dinner. As the main course."

"You used to like that, as I recall."

"I used to like a lot of things, Mitch."

He held her gaze and answered softly, "Oh, I don't think you've changed all that much, princess."

And for just a moment, looking into her eyes, watching that beautifully classic face that he knew as well as he knew the rhythm of his own breath, he was convinced that she hadn't changed at all. But even before his heartbeat could register surprise, the barrier slammed into place again, and her face was impassive. It was like looking at her through a block of ice.

"You stopped smoking," she said without much interest.

Mitch smiled. "Funny thing." He snapped the cigarette in two between the fingers of one hand and tossed it toward the ashtray. "Once I got rid of you, life seemed worth living again."

Diana gave him a saccharine smile. "Go away, Mitch," she said. "You obviously went to a great deal of trouble to crash this party, so go get your money's worth."

"What makes you think I'm not?"

She gave a graceful wave of her hand. "You're wasting your time with me. I'm beyond humiliation, shock or dismay. I lived with you too long. So go do what you do best. Insult innocent people, embarrass old ladies, enrage your hosts . . . just leave me alone."

"Don't worry, I'll get around to it. But right now I'm on break. If I dance with one more Shuge or Prue . . . where do they get names like that, anyway? Is there some kind of society dictionary—'Fifty Stupid Names for Baby Girls'?"

"Your break," Diana said deliberately, "is over."

Mitch extended his hand to her with a grin. "Dance with me, princess."

Diana drained the last of her champagne. "Not if you were the last man on earth."

He got to his feet, and his grin did not fade as he leaned close to her, cupping her cheek with his hand. "Don't drink so fast," he advised. "You know it gives you a headache."

Then he was gone, leaving her skin tingling from his touch and her head buzzing with a dozen unspoken retorts. Snappy exits were Mitch's forte. His snappiest, of course, had been the day he'd walked out on her.

Diana swallowed back a sudden bitter taste in her mouth and glared at her empty glass. Damn him, anyway. He was right—she was getting a headache. But it didn't have anything at all to do with champagne.

Chapter Five

She caught up with Etienne half an hour later.

"Darling," he said, catching her hands.

Diana knew immediately something was wrong, and with his next words he confirmed it.

"I am so sorry, but I must leave. I know it's early—"

"No," interjected Diana. "It's late. This party has been going on for days. Weeks. I'm more than ready to go home."

His smile was gently regretful. "You don't understand. I have to leave, but not just the party—the city. My flight leaves in less than an hour for Washington."

"Washington! But—"

He waved an impatient hand. "A very important countryman with a problem of documents. I knew I might be called away, but didn't expect it to be on such short notice."

Diana tried not to let her disappointment show. "I understand, of course. You won't be gone long?"

He slipped his arm through hers and turned her away from the crowd, bending close as he moved toward the wide set of double doors. The music had grown more romantic as the evening lengthened, the overhead lighting was dim and augmented by a synchronized sequence of soft pink, blue and green. "A few days, this time," he assured her.

And before she could pose the question, he supplied the answer. "But you should know, Diana, that there is a good possibility I will be reassigned—to Washington again."

For a moment Diana could do nothing but stare at him. *Perfect,* she thought. The perfect ending to a perfectly hideous day. Why had she expected anything better?

"I wasn't going to mention the prospect until I returned," he went on. "But now I think…" He smiled. "Haven't you another saying? Timing is everything?"

At the expression of confusion on her face, his levity faded. "Diana, my beautiful girl. I enjoy your companionship very much, you know that, don't you?"

She nodded. "And I enjoy being with you. But—"

"But," he agreed gently, "always between a man and a woman there comes a time when one must decide whether to go forward or not at all, isn't that so? And," he went on before Diana could interrupt, "I think you will not be ready to make that decision until you come to terms with another very important man in your life."

For a moment Diana genuinely did not understand. Then incredulity overcame her. "You can't mean—"

"Your husband," he said with a smile. "Who perhaps is not quite as 'ex' as you would like him to be."

She tried to tease him out of the absurdity. "Is that the well-known French jealousy talking? I wouldn't have believed it of you."

But he refused to be distracted, though his smile remained tender. "If I were jealous, it would be with good cause, I think." He raised a hand to forestall her protest. "I have observed the two of you for only a small space of moments, but even I see that the bond is still there." He gave one of those very expressive, very French lifts of his shoulders. "Some say anger and passion are mere reflections of each other. Perhaps it is so. Perhaps you need to discover precisely what it is that continues to bring the two of you together—or keeps you apart. And I think you will discover these things much better if I am not here."

Because he left her no choice, Diana said, "I see."

He bent and kissed her lightly on the lips. "You are a dear friend, Diana. I want only what is best for you."

Diana managed a smile. "If Washington is best for you," she said, "I'll miss you."

His lingering smile made her feel small and selfish for wishing he would stay. But he was wrong. The worst possible time for him to go away was now, while Mitch was here to plague and torment her. The last thing in the world she needed was private time with Mitch. What she needed was protection from Mitch, distraction from Mitch, reasons to stay away from Mitch....

The course of her thoughts startled Diana, for until Etienne had brought up the matter she had never realized how defensive she was on the subject of Mitch. But why was it that whenever things started going well for her, whenever it started to look as though she just might have a chance at a little scrap of happiness, Mitch was always there, as if on cue, to wreck it for her?

Etienne glanced regretfully at his watch. "Darling, I must go. I'll leave the car for you, *bien?*"

"Don't be silly." She forced a smile and straightened the crease of his lapel with an affectionate, maternal gesture. "The consulate car is for taking you to the airport, not for taking your date home from a party."

He looked doubtful. "Are you sure? I don't like—"

"One phone call and I can have a dozen cars lined up outside," she assured him. "And you're going to need those diplomatic tags to get you out of all the traffic tickets you're going to collect trying to get to the airport on time."

He smiled and took her shoulders. "Sometimes I forget what an independent woman you are. I'm not quite sure I like it, you know."

"It comes with the package," she informed him, and kissed his cheek. "You'd better hurry."

She was gratified to see the genuine regret in his eyes. "I *shall* miss you, Diana. I'll call you when I return."

"Goodbye, Etienne."

She could have stayed, of course, and perhaps as a courtesy to her hosts she should have. Under any other circumstances she might have. But it seemed to Diana that the evening had deteriorated to a point beyond salvaging; there was no point in waiting for outright disaster to strike before she finally admitted defeat and went home. Mitch seemed to be safely ensconced with a group of Texas oilmen—regaling them, no doubt, with tales of his mythological adventures in Arabian oil fields—and Diana decided there was no time like the present to make her escape. She delivered the requisite amenities to her hosts and went into her office to call for a car.

Until she met Mitch, displays of temper were simply not in her repertoire of modes of behavior. If there was one thing Mitch had done for her, however, it was to teach her there was a certain gratification to be had from kicking, cursing at, striking and otherwise abusing inanimate objects. She buzzed the concierge desk and told Evan to get her a car, then went to the file cabinet to get a folder she would need for tomorrow. But instead of retrieving the folder, she slammed the drawer with an oath and then kicked the side of the cabinet soundly.

"Dumped you, did he?"

Her private displays were not for public viewing, however, and hot, embarrassed color surged to her cheeks as she whirled around. She should not have been surprised to see Mitch leaning against the doorframe.

"This is a private office," she snapped. She turned away, adjusting the drape of her jacket at the shoulders, commanding her hot face to cool and her heart to stop pumping so quickly. "And he did not dump me, as you so elegantly put it. He was called out of town."

Mitch swung the door shut and moved into the office, glancing around casually. It was a very small room, carved from what Diana suspected had once been a storage closet, and he filled it up completely. "Not to criticize, babe, but didn't you at least rate a window?"

In fact, the hotel decorator had taken a cramped, awkward space and made it quite pleasant. A man with Mitch's crude sense of style could hardly be expected to appreciate that, however, so Diana chose to ignore him—or at least to ignore his comment. But ignoring Mitch's presence when there were less than four feet of usable space between them in any direction was a virtual impossibility.

She turned back to the filing cabinet and opened a drawer. "You look tired, Mitch. Why don't you go to bed?"

He picked up a small ceramic statue from her desk and examined it absently. "There's nothing worse than sleeping alone in a strange hotel, is there?"

Diana retrieved the file and closed the drawer, edging past him with a deliberately pleasant, distantly tolerant look. "I wouldn't know."

He arched an eyebrow. "And I'm not sure I want a clarification on that." He turned the little statue over in his hand. "What is this thing, anyway? It looks obscene."

"Everything looks obscene to you, Mitch."

He returned the statue to the desk. "It's an acquired skill. I could teach you if you want."

"There is nothing you could teach me that I would have the remotest interest in learning, as you have just proven for perhaps the hundredth time."

Mitch tried to repress a smile as he watched her skirt the entire width of the desk to avoid coming in contact with him. She had always been at her best when she put on that highbrow tone. He settled one hip comfortably on the edge of her spindly little desk and only hoped it wouldn't break with his weight.

"So," he said conversationally, "what's he got that I haven't?"

She pretended to be busy straightening the papers in the file. "Who?"

"Monsieur Rambo, or whatever his name is."

Diana frowned sharply. "Don't sit on my desk."

"That's not an answer."

Diana looked at him impatiently, recognizing the mood. Something was on his mind and to distract himself he would pester, prod and torment Diana until he got tired of the sport or found something better to do. Fortunately, his attention span was relatively short and the mood couldn't be expected to last long. But tonight Diana was not inclined to tolerate it for even a minute. She wasn't married to him any longer. She didn't have to tolerate anything.

"The name is Randolais," she replied calmly. "Etienne Randolais. It's French. Perhaps you've heard of it? The language of love?"

"Oh, I know a thing or two about French," he drawled in a tone just as pleasant as hers had been. "Some even go so far as to say I've achieved a certain—shall we say?—expertise in the area."

Diana abandoned the effort to keep her expression neutral. "You are a disgusting man."

He lifted one index finger slightly. "Another area in which I qualify as an expert."

Until Mitch actually walked into her office, he had not realized why he had followed her. Until that moment he had not realized that tonight was the first time he had ever seen her with another man. And the Frenchman was not just another man—he was smooth, sophisticated, good-looking and so perfectly matched with Diana that the two of them could have been charms on a bracelet. He had watched another man kiss his wife. He had watched another man put his hand on the small of her back in that familiar protective way. He had watched another man bend close and smile. And he had watched her smile back. He told himself it was only natural to be a little curious. But what he was feeling now was more than curiosity; it was a possessiveness that surprised even him with its sheer ferocity.

"What'd you guys fight about?" he asked casually.

"We didn't fight about anything at all."

"Oh, yeah? You're here by yourself and he's gone off somewhere by himself. Sure looks like the symptoms of a fight to me."

Diana eyed him coolly. The way he sat, with one foot resting on the floor and the other swinging before him, drew the material of his jeans taut across his thighs in a way that was impossible to ignore. Only a few hours ago he had been naked and she had been in his arms. Diana was amazed by the fact that he was even more tantalizing now, fully clothed, sitting on the edge of her desk and completely oblivious to the way the fit of his jeans outlined his shape and tightened her throat. His particular brand of raw sexual chemistry was not something that faded with time or dimmed with exposure. She had long since learned to accept that.

"That's the trouble with you, Mitch," she said. "The only way you know to solve any problem is to fight it out. Well, I'm sorry to disappoint you, but there are people in this world who are far more civilized than that."

He grinned.

He *had* noticed the way her eyes kept returning to his thighs, and she quickly jerked her gaze away.

"I guess nobody ever accused us of being civilized, did they, babe?" He said it as though it were something to be proud of. "We raised fighting to an art form."

"And look what it got us." Diana did not look at him, but pretended to busy herself by flipping through her appointment book. "A divorce."

He ignored that. "So what kinds of problems are you and Pretty Boy having?"

She gave up trying to look busy and eyed him dryly. "You'd love for me to say it was you, wouldn't you? Well, I'm so sorry, but you don't get to be the center of attention this time. It's only proof of Etienne's nobility of spirit that he was able to forgive me for having once had the bad taste to marry you."

Mitch shook his head slowly. "Nobility of spirit," he repeated. "That's just what a man needs to live with you. That, and a whip and a chair."

Diana looked at him thoughtfully. "Etienne said that there was still something between you and me. I'm beginning to think he was right."

"Murderous intent?" suggested Mitch.

"That's putting it rather nicely, as a matter of fact. Now if you'll excuse me . . ." She picked up her purse. "I was on my way out."

Mitch's knees were blocking her exit from behind the small desk, and she refused to go around the other way. She looked down at his legs deliberately but he chose to ignore her.

"So early? The party is just getting off the ground."

"Then you should go enjoy it. Let me by, please."

"Somehow it just won't be as much fun without you there."

"I can't tell you how sorry I am to have ruined your evening. But it seems to me that since you are supposed to be keeping a low profile anyway, the smartest thing for you would have been to stay in your room. Will you kindly get out of my way?"

"I like to live dangerously." Mitch got lazily to his feet, but instead of making room for her to get by, the movement only further crowded the narrow space behind the desk. His eyes took on a subtle gleam as he realized this. "Seems to me there was a time you liked it, too, or you never would've gotten hooked up with me."

He took a small step forward, and their chests were almost touching. If Diana had stepped backward, her shoulders would have been pressed against the side of the file cabinet. Of course, she did no such thing.

"So what do you say, Di?" Mitch said huskily. "You still like to live dangerously?"

Not so much as an inch separated them. If Diana had taken a deep breath, her chest would have brushed the lapels of his jacket. She could see the low firelight in his eyes, which was part subtle teasing, part genuine challenge. She could feel his warmth, smell his scent. Mitch did not wear cologne but he had his own unique scent, a combination of spicy soap and salty skin and simple, undefinable Mitch. It was as subtly erotic as the whisper of a fingertip across naked skin, and he was so close that her mouth watered in memory of the taste of him. Her heart was beating slowly, steadily. She looked at him for a long time.

Finally, she said, "Get out of my way, Mitch."

His smile was just a little slow in coming. "No problem," he said. "Getting out of your way is one thing I've had plenty of practice at."

He moved aside as much as the space would allow. She started to edge past him, and tripped trying to avoid stepping on his foot. He put his hands on her waist to steady her, and their eyes met.

It was an insignificant movement, an automatic gesture, the kind of thing a complete stranger might have done if a woman he had never seen before had stumbled trying to move past him. But when Mitch put his hands on her waist, it was more than the physical contact, it was the gesture and the ease with which he performed it that struck Diana as so intensely familiar, so *husbandly*. A wave of recognition so sweet it was almost a welcome went through her, briefly taking her breath away and closing off her throat. The sensation washed over her and was absorbed almost before she knew it, and she was left open, vulnerable... willing. *Damn,* she thought helplessly. And again, *Damn...*

She saw the slow dilation of his pupils as his eyes moved over her, down the front of her body from breasts to hips and back again. It was as though she could feel him taking her in, absorbing, tasting, savoring.

His awareness of her was a heavy, pulsating thing, pushing its way inside her skin. Her response to him was throbbing, electric, tingling. The air between them seemed to hum and shimmer. It was always like that when they touched. Always.

"Did you say something about my getting out of your way, princess?" he asked softly.

Her voice was steady, amazingly so. She held his gaze, and she didn't move. "You're a sexy man, Mitch," she said. "But the world is full of sexy men. It doesn't mean a thing."

"Yeah." He moved his hands lower, barely a whisper of a caress, tracing the shape of her hips and her outer thighs. "Just like the world is full of women with great legs and smart mouths. So go home, princess, before we're both sorry."

For a moment he almost thought he meant that. He almost convinced himself he meant it. But she stood there in the circle of his arms, filling the air with the subtle scent of that perfume whose name he could never remember, all silk and creamy textures, fiery diamonds and winter white—and he knew the last thing he intended to do was to let her go.

With perhaps only the hint of a waver in her voice, Diana said, "Let me by."

"Sure. No problem." He did not notice the slight hoarseness in his own voice.

He could feel it between them, static lightning so hot and quick it vaporized every particle of oxygen in the atmosphere, leaving nothing to breathe but Diana. She was a drug, toxic and intoxicating, that turned his blood into molten lead. Now, while at least part of his brain was functioning, was his last chance to step away. Now, before the rush of hormones left him completely senseless; now, before he lost himself totally in that blur of navy blue eyes and the spinning memories of taste and touch and exploding sensation....

Don't go, Di. he thought. And he didn't move.

Diana couldn't seem to look away from him, and after a moment she forgot why she should. The trouble with Mitch was that he was impossible to resist, like chocolate or salted nuts or sweet wine and firelight on a cold rainy night. Just a taste, just a touch, and before she knew it a moment turned into an hour, an hour into a night, a night into a lifetime.... She knew the temptation, she knew the danger. But it had been so long, and remembering how long it *had* been caused her heart to swell, to fill her chest so completely it could barely continue to beat. Just one touch. One taste....

Reason number three, she thought and, lifting her face, she swept her tongue across his slightly parted lips. She tasted salt. She tasted Mitch. The sensation sent a shiver of hungry anticipation through her, a tightening of greed deep in her stomach. She drew his breath into her mouth, hot and quick. She felt his fingers tighten and turn to steel on her waist, and it almost seemed she could feel his pulse throbbing in her veins, an erratic counterpoint to her own. He bent his head and pressed his mouth into her neck. Colors exploded inside her head.

Her evening purse dropped to the floor. Her hands went to his waist to steady herself and then dropped lower, shaping his buttocks and his thighs and then around, moving between his legs to the warm, dark secret heat that was cupped by the soft fabric of his jeans. She tightened her fingers and felt his swift indrawn breath, the flare of strength in his muscles, the stirring of power in her hand. She opened her mouth to the invasion of his.

Her knees were weak, her head was spinning, her entire awareness was a collage of impressions: dark eyes, steamy heat, harsh breathing; the sweep of his tongue on the lobe of her ear; the trip wires of sensation that exploded across the network of her nerves. She clung to him for support, fingers tightening on his arms as his lips closed on the flesh just above her breast, at the neckline of her dress. Perspiration sheened her body. Her heart roared like thunder. "Mitch," she whispered, "we can't... Don't..." But even as she spoke, her hands were tugging at his shirt, pulling it from his jeans.

"I know." Hot breath skated across her face, strong fingers cupped her buttocks and moved down, skimming her thighs. "I won't." His mouth covered hers.

Diana thrust her hands beneath his T-shirt, opening her fingers against hot, damp flesh, spreading upward into the tangle of silky hair and over the swell of chest muscles. She drank him in, dizzy from him, drunk on him, weak with the battery of sensation and the power of need.

With the ease of one to whom understanding her signals was second nature, Mitch supported her with one strong hand on the small of her back, pressing her close. His other hand caressed her leg just below the hem of her skirt, then moved upward, dragging the silky material of her dress up and over her thigh. Breathless, aching need swelled inside her, knotting into a low, tight pressure as his fingertips played over her skin, now pressing, now stroking, now tracing the gentle indentation the garter snap left in the flesh of her upper thigh.

Diana pressed her teeth against his neck, stifling a moan as his fingers toyed with the lace edging of her panties, teasing, tantalizing, building the ache into an agony. His breath, her breath. Heat so thick they seemed to be swimming in it. Diana drank of the skin of his neck, drawing his taste inside her mouth with a desperate, greedy hunger.

Her breath stopped as, without prelude or warning, his fingers slipped inside the silky barrier of her panties. With maddening, wondrous, consummate skill his fingers moved, stroking, gently pressing, caressing—tightening those fine wires of pleasure that twisted from his touch to her womb and from there to every part of her body. They were poised on the edge of the abyss, and she dimly realized that if ever there had been a point of no return, they had passed it long ago.

She could feel the sharp edge of the desk against her backside as he lowered her downward. She was breathless, quivering inside. The entire world had narrowed to the sharp focus of her need; her hands fumbling with the snap of his jeans, his hands pushing up her skirt, breaths rasping, heartbeats roaring....

And suddenly the world was shattered by a sharp raucous screech.

At first the sound barely penetrated Mitch's consciousness; he didn't even begin to recognize it. But Diana went stiff in his arms, her misty blue eyes a blur of shock and confusion, and the moment was gone. The sound came again, going through him like a knife, and with one distant, detached part of his vision Mitch saw the intercom light on Diana's telephone blinking. A short, vulgar oath escaped him on a breath.

Diana pressed weakly against his chest. Her voice was tight, unsteady, threaded with shaky breaths. "Evan...my car. I told him to buzz me."

Mitch was bursting for her, and the need was so intense it was like a pain going through him in waves. Perspiration prickled his forehead and dampened his hair. His skin was on fire. His body couldn't accept what his mind told him and he could have roared with frustration and need. Then he looked into Diana's eyes and he saw a reflection of his own agony that was even—impossibly—more intense.

She started to twist away from him, reaching for the phone.

"Leave it," he said hoarsely, holding her more closely.

"He'll come back here—"

Mitch kissed the dampness from her face, his hand stroking the inside of her thigh, moving upward to massage her belly.

Diana's heart pounded, choking off her breath. Every muscle in her body tensed with longing, nerves ready to explode. "Mitch, don't..." A near sob of frustration broke her voice. "Evan...there's no time...."

"I know." He circled her ear with his tongue, sending an electric rush of sensation through her. "Hush."

He pushed aside her panties and began again his easy, expert rhythm, stroking, caressing and thrusting inside. Her body responded without hesitation to his touch despite her mind's best advice, for he knew her secret pleasures, her most intimate vulnerabilities, and he manipulated them deftly and without shame. In only a matter of seconds the shudders of release broke over her, leaving her weak and dazed and gasping in his arms. There was a steady knocking noise in the background that she could not entirely place.

"Miss Moore?" The knocking came again. "Are you there?"

Mitch's lips brushed her hair and his breath was a soothing steady stream against her ear. She was too weak to move; the entire room seemed to pulse with the shattering beat of her heart.

"Okay?" Mitch whispered.

She nodded against his shoulder.

"Miss Moore?" The knocking again.

Diana lifted her eyes to Mitch's. After another moment she managed to call, "Yes! I—I'm on the phone."

A pause. "It's Evan. I'm sorry to bother you, but your car is here."

Diana pulled her gaze away from Mitch with a concentrated effort. "Thank you, Evan."

"Yes, ma'am."

She swallowed hard and moved away from Mitch, straightening her skirt, brushing at the wrinkles in her jacket. Her throat was tight. She didn't know what to say. She couldn't look at Mitch again.

Mitch bent and retrieved her evening purse from the floor. "You've got a little strand of hair," he said, gesturing, "there...."

She lifted her hands and quickly smoothed back her hair where he indicated. He handed her purse to her.

"Better fix your lipstick."

She did so, though she didn't do a very good job. She snapped closed her purse and turned to him, torn, uncertain. "Mitch..." Her voice sounded hoarse.

But his smile was light, his stance casual. His eyes revealed absolutely nothing. "I'll wait here for a while after you're gone," he said. "It wouldn't do for us to be seen leaving together, would it?"

"I..."

"'Night, princess."

In the end she had no choice. "Good night," she answered quietly. And she left.

Chapter Six

Mitch rode up in the elevator with a man he recognized as the same one who had followed him all afternoon: hatchet face, blank features, bad suit. At any other time Mitch would have been disturbed to realize that this was the first time he had noticed the man all evening—he was usually more alert than that—but by that time he was too disturbed even to care. He barely remembered which button to push, or where he was supposed to be going.

He glanced at the man who stood beside him. "You got a name?"

His companion stood with his eyes straight ahead, shoulders straight, unresponsive.

"Come on, man, if we're going to be spending this kind of quality time together, we ought to at least be introduced."

The other man was as blank faced as a palace guard.

The doors slid open on the third floor, but Mitch hesitated. He didn't know why he had gotten onto the elevator at all when what he really wanted was a drink. And not in the Zephyr Room, either. In some dark and noisy bar that smelled like cigarette smoke and grease, where the bartender couldn't even spell Mai Tai, much less mix one, and where fistfights were the only form of entertainment offered. Of course, in his current mood, he would probably end up in jail, but that wasn't why, when the door started to close, he pushed "Door Open" instead of "Lobby" and stepped out of the elevator. It had something to do with Diana, and he really didn't want to examine exactly what it was.

His companion exited the elevator with him but fell several paces behind as Mitch started down the corridor to his room. "I think I'll call you Harold," Mitch tossed over his shoulder to him. "Everybody's got to have a name, and you look like a Harold to me."

Mitch shook out a cigarette and brought it to his lips. Diana's scent, sweet and musky and rich, swept over him. Damn it all, anyway. Why had he let her go? What had gotten into him? He used to *take* what he wanted.

Maybe the problem was that he was no longer sure what it was, exactly, that he did want.

He looked at the cigarette for another contemplative moment, then put it between his lips. He glanced at Harold. "You got a match?"

The other man walked past him, toward the little parlor at the end of the corridor, without responding.

"Probably just as well," Mitch muttered. And he tossed the cigarette into a potted plant that stood against one wall. Diana would've hated that.

In his room he called for a bottle of bourbon, then stood under a cold shower until his lips started to turn blue. He pulled on one of the hotel's big terry robes, and thought of Diana, all steamy from a shower, wrapped in a fluffy white terry robe, and completely naked underneath. On her it had been as sexy as a negligee. Sexier.

It came back to him as though it had happened yesterday.

Caesar's Palace, Las Vegas. It had amazed him to learn that she'd never been there. She, who had lived all over the world, had never even visited the world's biggest playground. He had practically had to kidnap her to get her on the plane. She was furious, of course—and excited and intrigued and trying hard not to show it. And he, as always, loved to see her wrestling with her emotions. Finally, curiosity won out.

"Where are we going? Where are you taking me?"

"To the world's biggest carnival. A twenty-four-hour party."

She looked doubtful. "Rio? New Orleans?"
He laughed.

She had hated Vegas and loved it, been appalled by its tackiness and intrigued by its brashness and constantly astonished by its sheer audacity. No one had ever seemed more out of place in the midst of all the paste jewels and glittering spectacle—and no one had ever enjoyed it more. She won fifty dollars at a slot machine while Mitch lost three thousand at the tables. They had champagne breakfasts at three in the morning. He bought her a cheap plastic poodle with a rhinestone collar around its neck; she taught him, much to his amazement, to play faro.

And then she'd come out of the shower wearing nothing but that white terry robe and Mitch was suddenly aware that he couldn't picture the future without her. It happened just like that, from one moment to the next. He loved her so much. And he wanted her.

"Marry me," he said, "and the carnival will never end."

Even to him, even then, the proposal sounded embarrassingly corny. But six hours later she married him in a tacky little wedding chapel decorated with pink paper roses, and it had seemed like the most natural thing in the world to do.

Mitch caught himself standing still, one hand on the bottle of bourbon and the other on a water glass, completely lost in the memory. With an irritated scowl he poured a dash of bourbon into the glass and started to turn away, then thought about it, and filled the water glass to the top. It was going to be a long night, and he might as well do it right.

The bedroom curtains were open and the city of San Francisco was spread out before him, thousands of winking lights that curved over hills and dipped into the water. The Bay Bridge. The Coit Tower. The Bank of America building. Russian Hill, alight with a hundred tiny pinpoints. And did one of those lights belong to a woman who had once stood beside him in a paper-and-plastic wedding chapel and vowed to share her life with him?

Vows that meant nothing to her, just as they had meant nothing to him. Vows that they had been trying to break almost from the moment the last syllable was spoken. Vows that were impossible to break and redundant to make because from the very first minute they met, it was as though their bodies and souls had been polarized, magnetically bound together. They couldn't get away from each other no matter how hard they tried.

Mitch stood in front of the window, sipping his bourbon and watching the lights.

It was almost 1:00 a.m. She had to work in the morning. She would be asleep.

She wouldn't be asleep. She would be sitting in front of the fire with her favorite comfort foods, a bowl of butter-brickle ice cream and a glass of red wine. How many times had he come in at two or three in the morning, trying to muffle the sound of the door and his footsteps, only to find her just so, eating ice cream and drinking wine and trying to pretend she hadn't been crying. A stab of remorse went through him when he realized the times were too numerous to count.

This is crazy, he thought. *You never should have come here in the first place. Tonight you had a close call and tomorrow, if you've got any sense, you'll be on the first plane out of here. The last thing you want to do is take any more chances.*

He put the glass down and started pulling on his clothes. Three minutes later he left the room.

His shadow was nowhere to be seen, but Mitch knew from experience that appearances could be deceiving. "Yo, Harold," he called, dropping his room key into his pocket. "Let's move. We're going for a ride." *To hell and back, probably,* he added to himself wryly.

But he had never in his entire life done the smart thing, the wise thing, or the safe thing. And this was no time to begin.

FROM THE STEREO SPEAKERS came the soothing sounds of Haydn. Diana loved Haydn. She loved the way the firelight tossed golden reflections over the oak-paneled walls and muted the colors of the Persian carpet at her feet. She loved the feel of the worn velvet sofa on which she sat, so aged, so permanent.

She loved the taste of rich creamy ice cream and the warm mellow feeling two glasses of wine gave her. She sat in her nightgown before the fire, curled up in a corner of the camel-backed sofa, and thought she probably had everything any woman could want.

Then why was it all she could think about was what she didn't have?

Didn't have, she reminded herself sternly, and didn't want. But, oh, why did Mitch have to make it so hard for her to remember that whenever he was around?

He was like a disease, she decided, a viral infection for which there was no cure. It would flare up without warning at the slightest stimulus, resulting in fever, madness, and more....

The grandfather clock in the corner chimed one-fifteen. He would be drinking by now, in his room or in some bar. She hoped that when he'd left, he'd had sense enough to call a cab.

She knew that the memory of what had transpired between them in the office should bring a flush of hot shame to her cheeks, but it didn't. Viewed from the perspective of two glasses of wine and half a carton of ice cream, their encounter seemed . . . inevitable. Such was the power of the sexual chemistry between them that sometimes mere proximity could ignite the flame.

Yes, she would have made love to him there in her tiny office—where anyone might have walked in at any moment—and she would have done so without hesitation or regret. And yes, when they'd been interrupted, Mitch had seen to her satisfaction without giving any thought to his own. And that neither shocked nor surprised her. For Mitch, such generosity of spirit was only second nature.

Mitch. Her husband. She knew him too well. And he knew her even better.

She would not put herself through the pain of losing him again for anything this world had to offer. Then why was she sitting here thinking about him with a knot of longing in her chest that felt as big as the Hope Diamond? What was it about her that made her keep buying into the fairy tale of "maybe this time...?" What kind of fatal flaw in her psychological makeup made her keep wishing he was different, she was different, and that dreams could come true...? Why did she insist upon believing that it was possible to have it all?

Not that she'd ever believed, not for one minute, that Mitch was the answer to that dream. But sometimes when she thought about how close they had come, she could hardly breathe for the sorrow that filled her chest.

But not tonight. Tonight she was not going to sit here feeling maudlin over something that had been over long ago. She wasn't going to torture herself over something that should never have been. She'd made a mistake and she'd been punished for it—over and over again. It was time to let go, move on.

And she would, she was sure. Someday soon.

The clock chimed one-thirty. When she heard the doorbell ring she hesitated. Not because she was startled, but because it was inevitable.

She did not even have to check the security port to see who it was. She opened the door.

He stood on her doorstep only half-visible in fog and the soft yellow porch light, looking like something from a half-forgotten dream. His hair was damp, from the mist or from a recent shower, and its curls were soft and tousled. All of him seemed a little blurred at the edges, gentled by the night despite the fact that he was scowling faintly as he stood there, fingers thrust into the front pockets of his jeans.

Maybe it was the wine. Maybe it was the stillness of the hour, or the absurdly romantic way the fog billowed and curled around him, or that she had *known* he would come, she had only been sitting there, waiting for him.... But when she opened the door, and saw him there, everything within her seemed to open and blossom toward him, and she half expected him to sweep her into his arms and silently carry her away into the depths of her most erotic fantasies. She was even, for that single, dazed moment, on the verge of taking the step that would lead her into his arms.

Then, scowling, he said, "Don't ever do that again."

That was the trouble with Mitch. He never fit into the fantasy.

"Do what?"

"Open the door in the middle of the night without checking to see who's there."

"It's late, Mitch," Diana said wearily. "What do you want?"

The scowl faded. "Relax," he said. "Not what you think. Can I come in?"

Diana hesitated, then stepped away from the door. Her heart was still pounding uncomfortably, but mostly from irritation now. And perhaps disappointment. She stepped away from the door. "Why not? It's your house."

Mitch crossed the threshold.

She was dressed for bed in yards of what appeared to him to be cotton sheeting, white with a pale stripe, long sleeves, deep ruffle at her ankles. It was the kind of nightgown that would have been perfectly appropriate in a convent—except that the neckline was scooped so deeply that the garment appeared to be clinging to her shoulders by force of will alone. And when she moved, all that white material swayed and billowed and clung to the shape of the body underneath which, as she walked into the light, he could tell was completely naked. He was not prepared for that, and it struck him in that moment that the nightgown was a metaphor for everything that compelled him about Diana. He always thought he knew what to expect, and he was always wrong.

Her hair was down, wound into a flat, loose braid that framed her face with a few careless strands. It had been so long since he had seen her as anyone but Ms. Moore of the sleek chignons and stylish suits, he had almost forgotten the real woman behind the facade. Oddly, it was the sight of that girlish braid, even more than the silhouette of her unclothed body beneath the voluminous cotton, that caused a tightening low in his belly.

"Looks like the stuff my grandma used to use to cover feather pillows," he remarked.

"What?"

"The nightie."

"I never thought you were the kind to notice what a woman wore to bed—unless of course it was crotchless or edible."

"Don't I wish. Two hundred dollars on sale at I. Magnin, right?"

"What?"

"The nightgown."

They had reached the library and Diana turned to him with an impatient frown. "Oh, for heaven's sake,

Mitch, you didn't come all the way out here in the middle of the night just to criticize my wardrobe.''

He looked around absently. Somehow he had expected this room to be different, but she hadn't changed a thing. The same forest green on the walls—God, he had hated that color—the same faded Persian rugs she had scavenged from her mother's attic. Even the same strains of her favorite music. "Remind me to bring you something crotchless next time I come."

She had a fire going, and the bowl of ice cream on the sofa table was the approximate size of a soup tureen.

It had taken her a long time to get this room just the way she wanted it; for months she had done nothing but work on it. Why had he thought she would change it just because he was no longer there to share it with her?

Diana sat down in a corner of the sofa, picking up her wineglass and curling her feet beneath her. He sat on the other end of the sofa, picked up the bowl of ice cream and swung his feet onto the sofa table. Diana had to bite back an indignant objection. Did it really matter where he put his feet? Besides, the table was a reproduction.

The sofa wasn't very large and even though he sat on its opposite end, he was much too close. Diana had forgotten, in fact, how small the room was until he'd walked in. How was it that one man could make a room feel crowded just by entering it?

She could see the water droplets that clung to his hair, and on his neck, just above his collarbone, was an angry red bruise that alarmed her at first—until she realized it wasn't a bruise, that she had put it there. The intimacy of the memory, the visual evidence of what had passed between them only hours ago, caused a heavy warmth to flow through her; a tingling uncertainty tightened her stomach.

Diana watched as he took a spoonful of the softened ice cream, gazing into the fire as though that, and only that, were what he had come for. Perhaps it was. She never knew with Mitch. Never.

Then he said, "No, it's not."

She sipped her wine, not bothering to question. Still, she could feel her heart beating and she knew it wouldn't resume a normal rhythm until Mitch went away, if then.

Mitch took another spoonful of ice cream, still looking into the fire, and his expression was thoughtful as he explained, "It's not my house. It never was."

Diana was startled. "How can you say that? You loved this house!"

He shook his head slowly. "I only loved the fact that you loved it. I knew how much it meant to you, having a real house, a place to put down roots after spending your life traveling around the world, and I wanted you to have it. I thought it would make you happy."

It did, Diana wanted to cry. *It did make me happy. And not just because I loved the house but because you gave it to me. Because you cared enough to make my dream come true....* She wanted to say that, and so much more, but what difference could it possibly make now?

So she sipped her wine and replied, "I suppose it was too much to expect for you to meet me halfway in trying to make a home."

He made a derisive sound and scooped up more half-melted ice cream. "This isn't a home." He gestured with the spoon before sliding it into his mouth. "It's a damn museum. Your problem was you never learned the difference between a home and a hotel—which is not much of a surprise since you always did spend more time there than here."

"Little wonder. Until you moved out, the hotel was a great deal more comfortable than the—" she searched only briefly for the words "—combination battlefield and pigsty into which you had turned my home."

"See?" he shot back. "*Your* home. If I had a dollar for every time I heard that phrase..."

"That's hardly the point, is it, Mitch?" Her fingers tightened on the stem of the glass. "The problem was that you simply weren't *interested,* isn't that right?''

He looked at her for a long time. "Yeah," he said. "That's right. You kept trying to civilize me, and I hated that. However..."

He passed the bowl to her, which Diana accepted cautiously.

"You must have had some effect despite my best efforts," he continued easily, "because I'm here now, aren't I, instead of in some sleazy bar somewhere beating up a drunk I don't even know."

"I'm not entirely sure that's something I should be grateful for," Diana murmured.

He smiled, though it seemed a weary expression, and rested his head against the back of the sofa. "Ah, Di," he said softly. "We sure made a mess of things, didn't we?"

Diana looked at the melted ice cream in her spoon and could not bring it to her lips. Her throat was suddenly so tight she could barely swallow. "Yes," she said huskily. "We did."

His posture was relaxed, feet up, head back, and arms looped across his chest, his eyes lazily hooded as he watched the fire. No one but Diana could have sensed the tension that crept into his muscles and played the subtlest of undercurrents in his voice. She was riveted by it.

Without turning to look at her and in the same surface-casual tone, he said, "You wanted to know what I was doing here. Well, I'm going to tell you. It's a long story, so maybe you'd better pour yourself another glass of wine. Pour me one, too, while you're at it."

"The glasses are in the kitchen." That subtle, low-level tension of his had actually migrated to her own muscles, and she was not at all sure she wanted to hear what he had to say. Or maybe it was just the fact that he was here, so close, so sure, so real, after all this time....

"Never mind." He reached for the bottle. "I don't need a glass."

Diana snatched the bottle out of his grasp, filled her own glass and handed it to him. He smiled as he contemplated the rosy liquid.

"Good thing we didn't stay married," he observed. "We'd both be in detox by now."

"You always did drink too much." Her tone had slipped into wifely disapproval and she scowled. He didn't even notice.

"Drinking too much became a lot more fun when I realized how much it irritated you."

"Your maturity was one of the things I admired most about you."

He grinned. "We always did bring out the best in each other, didn't we, babe?"

"You were going to tell me why you were here," she reminded him, keeping her tone as disinterested as she could possibly make it.

"Right." He turned the wineglass until it caught the flames of the fire, and he watched the play of colors in the liquid for a moment. Then he lifted the glass and downed half its contents in one swallow. He spoke to the fire, without looking at her.

"You're right about one thing. I've always thought of myself as a happy-go-lucky kind of guy, never meant to be tied down, not much interested in 'things'...I mean, look at this carpet." He gestured with the wineglass; the contents sloshed dangerously but didn't spill. "The insurance adjuster said it was worth twenty thousand dollars. *Twenty thousand dollars.* That's more than my pop made in a year all the time I was growing up, and he raised five kids. I don't know what blows my mind more—that you'd actually put something like that on the floor, or that your mother had it rolled up in her attic somewhere, completely forgotten."

Diana was uncomfortable. "Mitch..."

"No, let me finish." He drank from the glass again, but still he didn't look at her. "This isn't about the fact that we come from two completely different worlds. We do, but that doesn't matter, it never did, because I never cared about Persian carpets or Queen Anne chairs or whether the silver is sterling or plate. I never even noticed, never thought it was important. I grew up in a house with nine people, most of them all talking at once, fighting, loving, driving one another crazy—and all of it at the top of their lungs. That was home to me, something that always had been and always would be, something that just *was*. I guess maybe..." He frowned, searching for words. "When something is that much a part of you, you don't even think about it, even when it's gone, because you carry it around inside your head. Inside your soul. The things that are important to you are the things you don't have, I guess."

He drained the glass. "I know I'm not making much sense. And me, the writer..." For the first time, he slid a glance toward her, and in it was a hint of his familiar self-mocking humor. "Or so some people say, anyway."

He leaned forward to refill his glass from the bottle she had left on the table beside his feet. The humor was gone, his voice was quiet. His gaze had returned to the fire. "I wasn't interested in being domesticated, and it never occurred to me that a family—a home—was something you had to build. Somebody else had always done it for me, and they made it look easy. So it wasn't important to me."

He shrugged, and drank again from the glass. "Not that you were a big help, by the way. You knew about as much about being a wife as I did about being a husband, and the two of us trying to do something as conventional as making a home was nothing but the blind leading the blind. The difference was that it mattered to you, as much as you tried to pretend it didn't. It never mattered to me, because I would've loved you whether I'd ever married you or not. Home was just a place to hang my metaphorical hat.''

He took another sip. His eyes looked straight ahead. ''And then two days ago I came home one night to find home wasn't where I'd left it six hours before. Home was a strip of crime tape and a pile of smoldering embers and for the first time in my life I had nothing, and it *mattered*. And when I didn't have any place left to go, I thought about San Francisco, not because it was home, but because you were here.''

He drained the glass and set it on the table. Then, at last, he looked at her. ''I just wanted you to know that,'' he said. ''That's all.''

Diana focused her eyes on the bowl of melted ice cream on her lap. *Don't do this, Mitch,* she thought, and her shoulders were aching with the effort of holding herself stiff, closing him out. *Damn you for doing this....*

It was almost as though he read her mind, but that didn't surprise her, either. ''So that's my story, babe.'' He swung his feet to the floor and stood with his familiar easy swagger, and whatever sentimentality he had allowed to creep into his tone was banished with the gesture. "And in case you're wondering, no, this doesn't mean I'm ready to be civilized. It doesn't mean anything at all except you asked, and I told you."

"We never talked about—what went wrong," she said, in a very low tone.

The tape on the stereo chose that moment to click off, and Mitch didn't move. The silence between them was so charged it practically crackled.

Then Mitch said softly, "Ah, babe." His smile was quiet and sad and so tender it broke her heart. "Do we even have to?"

After a moment, she shook her head. It would have been easier to talk about what went right.

Diana put the bowl on the table. She stood, too. *Don't do this,* she thought. *I am not going to do this....*

Struggling for just the right measure of detachment, she said, "I hope you're not planning to drive back to the hotel."

If she had said nothing at all, or even if she had said something sensitive and caring and completely inappropriate, Mitch would have found it possible to shrug the entire past half hour off. But when she did that— when she squared her shoulders like that and looked straight into his eyes and tried so hard to be distant and untouched—he knew her too well, and it went straight to his heart. Before he knew it, he had reached out, and cupped her neck in what was meant to be a light, affectionate gesture.

"I hope you aren't going to ask me to stay."

Until he touched her she was quite sure she was going to be able to let him go. She intended to remove his hand. "No," she said firmly. "Of course not." But her fingers just closed on his arm.

She could see his eyes darken with a low restrained fire as he looked at her, moving quickly up and down, over her face, her breasts, her lips, her eyes. There was an almost imperceptible tightening of his fingers on the back of her neck, and his warmth melted into her.

"I didn't come here to make love to you, Diana." His voice was husky, strained with the war between honesty and the raw hunger she could see in his eyes. "God knows, the last thing I want to do is go to bed with you when it never stops there, when it's never enough, when it's nothing but poison for both of us, and you know that, Di."

Diana nodded. She could feel the pulse in her throat and the reverberation of her heartbeat, echoing throughout her body. Why didn't he just leave? Why had he come here at all, now, tonight, when wanting him was like a gnawing in her belly? It wasn't just wanting sex, it was wanting *him,* the one thing she could never have. Had he come only to remind her of that? Why didn't he just go away, now before it was too late?

And then he dropped his hand from her neck, and moved his eyes toward the door. "Get some sleep, babe. I'll catch up with you tomorrow."

Yes, Diana thought. *Yes, go now....* She was dizzy with the sudden absence of his touch and her chest hurt with the slow, squeezing force of her heartbeat. He was leaving. She followed him into the foyer.

He paused and looked at the spiral staircase. "You know why I always hated that thing so much?" He looked at her, and the familiar cocky smile was on his lips.

"Why?"

"Because I could never carry you up it. Spirals aren't very romantic, are they?"

Diana held his gaze, and he didn't look away. "How do you feel about walking?" she asked.

He said nothing. The moments seemed to tick off forever. And then he held out his hand.

Chapter Seven

Diana looped her arms around Mitch's neck. He could feel her heartbeat, hard and steady, and the curve of her breast against his chest. He turned his face to her arm and lightly kissed the soft inner flesh where the sleeve of her nightgown had ridden up. He released a breath. His voice was hoarse. "Diana, this is crazy. Why are we doing this?"

But her eyes were as luminous as twin moons in the misty darkness, steady and certain. "Because," she said, "we deserve this. After all we've put each other through, all the torment we've suffered, we deserve this one night."

Mitch put his hands on her waist. His fingers closed around handfuls of clean soft cotton, his knuckles brushed the curve of her waistline where it met the flare of her hips. At that moment he thought he could be perfectly content to stand there forever in the circle of her arms and just breathe.

He lowered his forehead to hers. He filled his eyes with her. He let her flow right into his skin. "I promise you," he said huskily, "you'll regret this."

Diana let her hands slide down the front of his chest. Deftly her fingers unfastened the snap of his jeans. "I already do," she answered.

But the truth was that the things she now regretted were the only things worth remembering, and the best mistakes of her life were the ones she had made with Mitch.

She felt his sharp intake of breath as she lowered the zipper of his jeans and pulled them downward, the tensing of his stomach muscles as she slipped her fingers inside the elastic of his briefs and tugged them down. Both garments pooled around his ankles, and he kicked them aside. Diana dragged her hands upward again, rediscovering him by touch—the sharp bones of his ankles, the feathering of hair over his calves, the flat muscles of his thighs.

She leaned forward and placed a kiss on the inside of his thigh, tasting him with her tongue. Her hands stretched upward, closing on his buttocks, then pushed beneath his sweatshirt, pressing the length of his back, his ribs, his waist. All the while her tongue circled upward, teasing him. His scent, faintly feral, intensely sexual, seemed to penetrate her skin and mix with her blood, making her light-headed with wanting.

His fingers closed on her shoulders, not guiding, not protesting, not urging, just communicating his pleasure. Now she was in control; soon he would have his turn. For in this one area of their shared life, symbiosis was as natural as the beating of a heart, and the sharing was complete and unquestioned. He took slow deep breaths and his pleasure spiraled through her, quivering electric currents, as if it were her own. With her hand she circled his hard, strong length and felt power throb in her fingers.

His fingers tightened on her shoulders with the quickening of his breath, the moan of pleasure buried deep in his throat. Her head swam with the thrill of his reflected pleasure. She wanted to drink him in, to take his pulse of life inside her own veins, to make him a part of her. The pores of her skin strained with wanting him, yearning to blend with him; her brain was filled with nothing but awareness of him. It was like coming home. Every plane and contour of his body was familiar to her, every variance of texture and taste, and yet all of it was new, as exhilarating and dizzying and breath-robbingly powerful as the first time. Her husband, her lover. The fever was inside her soul, the wonder of his nearness blossomed through her and left her weak.

His hands slipped beneath her arms as she straightened, tasting his nipples with the flat of her tongue, pressing a kiss into the hollow of his throat. With growing urgency, she swept her tongue across his collarbone, his neck, the lobe of his ear, tasting him, kissing him, drawing him in. His breath roared in her ear. His heat flared through her. His mouth covered hers. He swept her into his arms.

Mitch did not remember crossing the room, tumbling to the bed. They sank into the downy softness of an overstuffed comforter and it was like drowning in a cloud. His arms and legs tangled in yards of cotton nightgown; her supple flesh yielded against his hardness; her mouth, with the texture of velvet and the taste of heated wine, opened beneath his. He was drunk on her, helpless, reeling with sensory overload. No part of him was left untouched by her. The very air was syrupy with her presence, thick and hard to breathe. Yet each breath sent a new rush of the intoxicant that was her to his brain, wonder surged through him in waves that alternated with a need so intense his very skin seemed to cry out for her.

He couldn't get enough of her—her taste, her touch, silky limbs and porcelain skin, her honey-colored hair, loosened from its braid by the thrust of his impatient fingers, tangled on the pillow beneath him. Her hands pushed his sweatshirt up and he discarded it impatiently, his skin prickling for a brief moment from the temperature of the room but almost immediately lost in fever again as he sank into her embrace.

He caught handfuls of her nightgown and pulled it up over her head and her arms, losing it in the tangle of bedclothes around them. Then she was naked against him, long legs, rounded hips, the swell of her breasts. For a moment all he could do was hold her, his arms and legs enfolding her and pressing her close, covering himself with her, filling himself with her.

His hands began to move, stroking her thighs and the slim line of her waist, cupping her breasts, filling his hands with them. Her nipples were small and round, their shape and taste exquisitely familiar to him, intensely beautiful. She gasped and strained against him when he encircled her nipple with his tongue, drawing it inside his mouth, and he could feel the need that was tightening inside her because it was his own.

She tossed her head against the pillow, lifting herself against him, caressing his hip with her knee. He wanted to enter her then, to bury himself inside her and lose himself in the surcease of hunger she offered, but greed was an even stronger force, and he wanted more of her, for her pleasure and his were one and the same.

He caught her knees on either side of him and moved downward, sliding his tongue along the midline of her torso, dipping into her navel, pressing a deep, long kiss low on her abdomen. With his tongue he penetrated the damp heated crease at the juncture of her thighs and moved even lower, separating the folds of her most secret flesh, tasting, kissing, caressing. She writhed beneath him; through the roar of his own pulse he distantly heard her gasp his name. It was by instinct not design that he knew the precise point of her fulfillment, the instant before pleasure turned to pain, where urgency escalated to explosive demand. He knew it because he felt it within himself, the fire that suddenly surged out of control, the madness that was the overpowering, intensely focused need for her. Not just the need for that one compelling act of sexual completion, but the need for *her*. Only with Diana had he ever known the difference.

He wanted to enter her by inches, to sink into her with nothing more than the inexorable forces of gravity, savoring each sensation. He wanted to watch her eyes widen as she felt him filling her; he wanted to feel her breath still. He wanted that glorious rush of power held in check, of pleasure stretched to its finest, most attenuated extension; he wanted to watch, he wanted to feel, he wanted to memorize with every pore of his body the moment the two of them became one.

But there was that point when what they became together was, as always, more powerful than either of them alone.

His fingers thrust into her hair, and he took her muffled cry in his mouth as he plunged inside her. Dimly he felt the sharp bite of her fingernails on his back as she thrust to meet him, and a shock wave of sensation rocked him as he settled even deeper inside her.

He thought about solar flares, about storms at sea, about winds that swept away the faces of continents, but none of it came close to what he felt when he was in Diana's arms. Their coming together was a conflagration, a wild consumption of urgency and madness that had no rhyme or reason, only him, only her and the powerful need that drove them both. He could not get deep enough inside her or have enough of her against him; he wanted to bury himself inside her forever, he wanted to *become* her. He wanted to draw her breath into his lungs, feel her blood inside his veins, see through her eyes, he wanted to possess her. And again there was that curious split awareness, as there always was with Diana: the fierce, primitive, sexual need with its simple, all-consuming goal, and the deeper, more powerful spiritual need that compelled him with a longing so fierce he could hardly bear it— the need for Diana, the one thing he could never have, and the only thing he could not live without.

And for a moment, always for just that moment— as she strained against him and he felt her muscles begin to convulse around him, as the top of the world exploded and he held himself deep inside her while his very soul spilled out—in that moment when she opened herself to him completely and they clung together through the terrifying, exhilarating tumble into the abyss, then she was his and he was hers, without beginning and without end. It was only a moment, but eternity was composed of just such moments. And in that moment, and only then, he knew what living was for.

He did not know how long they lay together, arms and legs and breaths entangled, drifting, still, content. Colored lights and pulsing darks swirled against the screen of his closed eyes, and he wanted nothing more in his whole life than to lie there in the circle of her warmth, infused with her. When he thought of how long he had been without her, how close he had come to never knowing this wonder again, a swell of emotion tightened inside his chest that was so intense it hurt.

After a very long time, he got up and made his way to the bathroom in the dark. Parting from her was agony, and her hands trailed after him as he left the bed, urging him back. He returned in only a few moments with one of her big fluffy towels and began gently drying first her body, then his own. Her arms were reaching for him as he tossed the towel aside. He slid into her embrace again, his fingers stroking her wet, tangled hair.

He dropped a kiss onto her forehead. "I wish," he said softly, "I could tell you how you make me feel without sounding like a perfume commercial."

He felt the gentle curve of her smile against his chest. "And you, the writer," she murmured.

"Yeah," he whispered, bringing her fingers to his lips. His throat was too tight to say more.

He made his living with words—hard words, crisp words, precise descriptive words. But his was the soul of a soldier, not a poet. He could construct a chase scene so vivid hearts would still be pounding an hour after the last page had been turned. He could write dialogue so sharp and true that it could send chills down the spine of even the most seasoned reader. But when it came to telling the only woman who mattered what she meant to him, he was reduced to fumbling clichés and hackneyed phrases. Then he wished he were a poet. Then he wished he were anything else in the world except what he was—the man who wanted, and could not have.

He kissed her hair again and patted her hip lightly. "Sit up for a minute, babe."

He tugged at the covers beneath them. She murmured a protest but shifted her weight, allowing him to turn down the bedclothes. "Your bedspread is ruined, you know."

"Comforter."

"Whatever. Looks expensive."

"You're such a materialist."

"You know I married you for your money. Come on, get under before you catch a chill."

He held the covers up for her and Diana wriggled beneath them, into the warmth of his arms again. It struck her then what a husbandly thing that was to do, how protected and sheltered and *married* it made her feel. Warm and naked in the arms of her husband and lover, listening to the strong, steady beat of his heart, snug beneath an eiderdown comforter.... These were the moments that had always come too rarely, moments that were so nearly perfect it hurt deep inside to even think about them. These were the moments she wanted to last forever. And they never did.

She had known from the beginning of this night that the pain of letting him go would, in the end, outweigh even the pleasure they shared. She supposed in a way she had known that from the first minute she had allowed herself to fall in love with him. She told herself she could handle it, and she would. But not just yet. Her body was sore and her muscles were aching, but she could not have enough of him. She slipped her hand between his thighs, stroking him to readiness again. His breath began to quicken, he grew hard in her hand, and when he whispered, "Diana," she stilled his lips with her own.

"Why," he murmured as they moved against each other, "do I get the feeling I'm being used?"

"Hush." She drew him down, holding her breath for the one long, exquisite moment as he pressed into her. "Oh, Mitch," she whispered. Her arms tightened around him until her muscles trembled. "I just want to feel you inside me. I just want..." She couldn't finish. *Too much,* she thought. *With you, I always wanted too much....*

Mitch held her close, kissing her face, drying the dampness with his breath. "I know, babe," he said softly. And he did.

Much later they fell into the sleep of exhaustion, still joined. When Mitch awoke after the first real sleep he had had in close to three days, an early-afternoon light was streaming over the bed, and Diana was gone.

Chapter Eight

Diana arrived at the St. Regis a little after eleven. Elise greeted her with a raised eyebrow. "What are you doing here so early?"

Except for Thursdays, Diana's usual hours were from 1:00 to 9:00 p.m. Check-in time was at three, and she had discovered that most problems involving VIP guests were likely to occur during the evening hours— an impromptu cocktail party, missed dinner reservations, an emergency request for theater tickets. It wasn't that she didn't trust the concierge staff to handle minor problems, but she liked to be on hand, just in case. The hotel had rhythms, a life force of its own, and Diana had learned to accommodate herself to those rhythms.

"Looking," Elise went on perceptively when Diana didn't answer, "if you'll pardon me for saying so, like . . ."

The understanding that dawned in Elise's eyes was far too accurate for Diana's taste, and Diana deliberately moved past the concierge desk toward her office. Elise followed.

"Like a woman who either had a very bad night," Elise persisted, "or a very *good* one."

"Honestly, Elise, you have the most single-minded imagination of anyone I've ever known."

Diana stepped into her office—and the memories were almost overwhelming. She was quite sure that if Elise had looked into her face at that moment, she would not have had to speculate; she could have read everything she wanted to know as clearly as newsprint. There was even an instant, when Diana first stepped into the room, that she thought she caught a hint of Mitch's scent, lingering in the air, and for just that instant it was so clear her stomach tingled in response. Diana turned quickly and slipped out of her lightweight swing coat, hanging it on the brass coatrack behind the door.

"That may be," agreed Elise, enjoying herself, "but if I were called upon to place a bet, I'd say I was looking at a woman who didn't leave the party alone last night. And furthermore, that the man she left with did *not* have a French accent."

"You're really bordering on bad taste, Elise." Diana picked up a stack of mail and began sorting through it.

Elise sat on the edge of the desk, nudging Diana with her shoulder. "But am I right?"

To Diana's great relief, the telephone rang just then. Before answering, she replied, "I'm not at all sure it's healthy for anyone to take such vicarious pleasure from the sexual exploits of others." She lifted the receiver. "Diana Moore."

"My office, Ms. Moore." And that was all. The voice was unmistakable.

Diana returned the receiver to its cradle with a bracing breath. "Mr. Severenson," she said. "I've been summoned. Excuse me." She squeezed past Elise toward the door.

"I live in San Francisco," Elise called after her. "Vicarious pleasure is the only kind I can get!"

Diana wasn't worried about why the hotel manager had requested her presence so brusquely; Rolf Severenson made a point of calling each of his executives on some minor infraction at least once a week as a way of opening up a dialogue—or, in Diana's opinion, a method of continually reasserting his authority. Diana had learned to enjoy their little confrontations. Today, in particular, she was glad to be called out of the office. She was glad for anything at all that would take her mind off Mitch.

It had required all of her resolve to leave him while he slept. She still felt raw and bruised inside, as though some vital part of her had been torn away and left behind with him. She knew she hadn't faced the worst, of course. She would have to see him at least one more time, and she didn't have the faintest idea what to say to him. She didn't even know what she *wanted* to say.

And that was why nothing that Rolf Severenson could say or do to her today could disturb her. She had a great deal more to dread than anything he could concoct.

The manager of the St. Regis had a corner office, as big as a small suite. The wallpaper was silk, the carpeting plush, the draperies damask. *Someday...* thought Diana.

Severenson was standing by the window, drinking coffee from a Wedgewood-patterned cup, when Diana came in. He nodded without inviting her to sit down.

"Ms. Moore," he said. "Is there any doubt in your mind as to who is in charge of this hotel?"

"No, sir," Diana answered.

He hesitated, his eyes narrowing slightly. "Who *do* you think is in charge, may I ask?"

Diana repressed a smile. "You are, Mr. Severenson."

He gave a curt nod. "Precisely. And does the phrase 'chain of command' mean anything to you?"

Diana didn't answer, growing impatient with the game.

"I cannot think of any circumstances whatsoever when it would be appropriate for the director of guest relations to give orders to the front desk about billing. The next time *you* think it's appropriate that a guest be billed for—shall we say, a broken vase of flowers?—you might suggest the same to Mr. Hollings, who is your direct superior. He, and not you, will make the final decision. Is that clear?"

Diana nodded. "Yes, of course. On the other hand, if it wasn't my place to suggest—" she emphasized the word slightly "—that the guest be billed, the front desk might have checked with Mr. Hollings."

"So they might have. But you have a way of giving orders that leaves very little room for debate, as you know very well."

With a gesture, Severenson invited her to help herself to coffee, indicating the reprimand was at an end, or at least at intermission.

"Would you like yours warmed?" Diana asked.

"Please."

He extended his cup, and Diana filled it.

"You want my job, don't you, Ms. Moore?" he inquired pleasantly.

Just as pleasantly, Diana replied, "Yes, I do."

"Well, you're not going to have it." He stirred his coffee with a silver spoon. "Not for another twenty years, anyway. By that time you may be qualified for the position."

"By that time I rather imagine you'll be more than glad to give it to me." Diana sat on the small love seat on the wall opposite the desk and crossed her legs.

"I wouldn't doubt that you're right." He sat, absently stirring his coffee. And he added in an offhand, purely conversational manner, "You were once married to Mr. DeSalvo, weren't you?"

Diana stiffened. Rolf Severenson might like to pretend to distance himself from his staff, but his mind was like a computer, filing away every detail, personal and professional, of every man or woman who had ever worked for him. He knew perfectly well Diana and Mitch had been married. He knew when, where, for how long and, most likely, how and why it ended—which was something neither of the two principal parties involved was prepared to say. He had never, ever raised the subject of Diana's personal life before. She could not imagine why he was doing so now.

Trying not to overreact, Diana replied carefully, "That's right."

"An interesting fellow. Did you know he once spent time in Attica? Not as an inmate, researching a novel. But of course you knew."

Diana had never heard that one. Her muscles wound another notch tighter. "I'm afraid he must have been pulling your leg."

"No, I read it in the *Times Book Review* not too long ago. Interesting article."

"I can assure you," Diana said firmly, "Mitch DeSalvo—by that or any other name—has never been reviewed in the *New York Times*."

Severenson lifted an eyebrow. "You are a snob, aren't you?"

"Yes," replied Diana evenly. "I am. That might even be one of the reasons you hired me, I suspect."

He chuckled softly. "Could be. Do you mind if I ask whether the two of you have any plans for the future?"

The question was so unexpected, so out of character and, considering the events of the past twenty-four hours, so incredibly badly timed that Diana could for the longest time do nothing but stare at him. Then she said, "Yes. I do."

She put the coffee cup aside and stood. "Thank you for the coffee. Good day."

"Where do you think you're going?"

Diana turned, feigning surprise. She was burning with humiliation inside but outside she was cool and controlled and as deliberately pleasant as ever. "I assumed the interview was over. You've delivered your weekly reprimand, engaged in the requisite three minutes of small talk, pried into my personal life and insulted me. Wasn't that all that was on the agenda for this morning?"

"Good Lord, no wonder he divorced you." Severenson's face reflected mild irritation and nothing more. "Sit down. Finish your coffee. The subject of ex-husbands is closed. I'd now like you to satisfy my curiosity on another no doubt sensitive matter."

Diana resumed her seat cautiously. Something very unusual was going on. Why did she suspect it had something to do with Mitch? Or perhaps it was simply that in her mind, whether she liked it or not, the entire world would for the next several weeks or more, exist for her only as it related to Mitch.

"Why are you working here?" Severenson asked.

Diana took a sip of her coffee, watching him. "Is that your subtle way of questioning my financial situation?"

"Of course not. That would be vulgar." He waited for an answer.

"My parents are well-off," Diana answered. "I'm not. I have a small trust fund, but I need to work."

"Otherwise bye-bye Mercedes and Aldopho originals, hmm?" Diana drew a breath to reply, but he waved her silent. "No, that was rude and I don't expect an answer."

He drank from his cup, silent for a moment, but his eyes remained on her. Then he said, "You have a lot of style. I guess you know that. Too much for this business. Long hours, low pay, and Lord knows it doesn't get better with seniority. I always wondered what attracted you to the business—but then, I wonder that about myself, too.''

He took another sip of his coffee. ''There's an opening for an assistant manager at the Dansier in New Orleans,'' he said abruptly. ''I'm prepared to recommend you for the position.''

It was not often that Diana was rendered speechless. Severenson had managed to accomplish it twice in the space of five minutes, and he had every right to be proud of himself. He was, however, much too well schooled to show it.

Diana knew she had to say something. All she could manage was to repeat in a slightly dazed tone, ''The Dansier.''

''It's not the St. Regis, of course.'' Severenson shrugged. ''A small hotel, still somewhat inconsistent, but a good place to grow and learn. Certainly New Orleans is not a venue to be ignored. And if you do well within the company...'' He let the sentence finish itself.

Diana's head reeled. Of course she knew the Dansier. It had recently been taken over by one of the most successful management chains in the world and had only last year earned its first four-star rating. Of course, it still had a long way to go toward earning its reputation in the industry, but Diana could be part of making that reputation.

"Of course, I'm quite the fool for doing this," Severenson went on. "No doubt you're surprised. You're an asset to the St. Regis, and it's well-known that I like to hold on to my assets." Again he shrugged. "But it doesn't hurt to have favors owed in this business, and the more strategically placed those favors are the better. That's another thing you'll learn. And I will tell you this, Ms. Moore. If you stay here, you will stay here, literally, in your present position, until you retire. You have made yourself far too valuable to leave us any latitude, which was your first career mistake. If you really do have ambitions toward my job, you have to get out. And the Dansier is the place to start."

Very carefully, Diana placed her cup aside and got to her feet. She extended her hand. "Thank you, Mr. Severenson. I'll need some time to think about it."

He shook her hand. "Don't take too long. There are at least a dozen young hotshots nipping at your heels, and time waits for no one—not even in New Orleans."

DIANA WAS STILL in a state of stunned disbelief when she reached her office. When she'd started out for Rolf Severenson's office, she had been so certain that nothing could disturb the equilibrium of her day more than the man who was even now asleep in her bed had already done. She had been wrong.

New Orleans. The Dansier. Assistant manager. It was possible. Until now it had been a dream she'd barely even acknowledged to herself, but suddenly, it was actually possible.

Diana had not been raised to work, nor had she been trained for any useful occupation whatsoever. Her mother believed women of their social strata should limit their ambitions to marrying well and giving tasteful parties; her father believed in the unqualified greatness of his offspring regardless of gender. The inevitable mixed signals had resulted in a woman with the ambitions of a brigadier general and the qualifications of a maître d'. Diana loved both her parents dearly, but she sometimes resented them for that.

Diana had long since given up hope that they would come to respect her career choice or accept her lifestyle, but she would have liked them at least to *recognize* both. And when she thought about the title "assistant manager," she had to admit her parents weren't far from her mind. She did not expect to impress them. She would never do that as long as she stayed in the hotel business, but an assistant manager was not easy to ignore. Assistant manager—second in command—of a four-star hotel in New Orleans.... That was significant. That was an accomplishment. That was indisputable proof that she was serious, and perhaps the most important person she needed to prove that to was herself.

Suddenly she wanted to talk to Mitch. He would have understood. He was the only person who had ever understood how she felt about her job. He didn't always like it and, on more than one occasion, he had used it against her, but he *understood*. More importantly, he had an incredible capacity for making her understand how she felt about things, for making her see any issue in a new light. But the last thing she could afford to do now was talk to Mitch, particularly about something this important.

Elise knocked lightly on her open door. "Excuse me, but who do we know who can get a selection of after-five gowns over here in the next hour—size eighteen?"

Diana grimaced. "Mrs. Rolander?"

Elise nodded. "Apparently she's not happy with what she packed for her husband's award banquet tonight, and I can promise you whatever she chooses is going to need some alteration, so we have to move quickly."

"Call Karen Sims at Overtime in Ghiradelli Square. Tell her to sew some size-eighteen tags into some size-twenty-two gowns and save us all some time."

Elise gave her an admiring look. "Guess that's why they pay you the big money. So as long as you're on a roll..." She consulted her notepad. "Housekeeping is ready for you to inspect the Crane Suite."

"Yes, of course." Diana gazed at the paper with assumed interest, but the truth was she had barely heard what Elise had said.

Elise looked at her questioningly. "You okay?"

Diana drummed her pencil point absently against the spotless desk blotter. "Did you ever hear that saying, 'You can have a great house, great job and great sex life—but not all at the same time'?"

"Oh, no." Elise's expression fell dramatically. "You got canned."

Diana shook her head, gazing at the random pattern of dots on the blotter. "Quite the opposite, as a matter of fact."

"My God!" Elise's eyes widened and she sank abruptly to the small chair beside the door. "You're having an affair with Mr. Severenson!"

That got Diana's attention, and her eyebrows drew together in disapproval. "Of course not. The truth is, he offered to recommend me for an assistant manager's position in New Orleans. The Dansier."

Elise was silent for a moment. Then she said carefully, "Just to be clear on this. You're *not* having an affair with Mr. Severenson."

"Don't be absurd."

"And your gorgeous Frenchman?"

Diana felt a stab of remorse as she realized how very little thought she had given to Etienne since he had said goodbye. Was she that fickle? Or had Mitch finally robbed her of the last shred of rationality she possessed?

"He was called away," she answered uncomfortably. "But I hardly see what that has to do—"

"Then who *are* you having this great sex life with?"

"Oh, Elise, for heaven's sake! You do have a one-track mind. I'm trying to tell you that I've been offered the job of a lifetime—"

Elise grinned. "I heard that part, sugar. Just trying to make sure you keep things in perspective, that's all. Congratulations. It sounds great."

Keep things in perspective. . . . The words echoed in her head. She did not know why they should bother her so. She *was* keeping things in perspective. This job was a dream come true, a gift from heaven, something that only an hour ago she had not even known existed. Severenson was right. If she stayed in San Francisco, her career was at a dead end. Why was she even hesitating?

She glanced at Elise. "Aren't you even surprised?"

"At the job? No. God knows you're qualified. That Severenson would recommend you—yes, a little. But I always did figure if he could find a way to get rid of you without doing himself any major damage, he'd take it."

"I suppose," Diana murmured, and it was with some surprise that she realized Elise was right. She *was* qualified. She could do that job. She really could.

Elise looked at her closely. "So what's bothering you?"

Diana began drumming her pencil on the blotter again. "Nothing really. I mean . . . I'm not sure."

"Of course it's hard picking up and moving to a new town—"

Diana gave a short laugh. "Heaven knows, I've had enough experience at that! I'd hardly call that a deterrent."

"And then there's Etienne. . . ."

Diana made a dismissing gesture with her wrist. He would not let her stand in the way of his transfer, and she wouldn't expect him to, any more than she would let him stand in the way of hers. They had simply never reached that level of commitment to each other. And until last night, Diana had not even wondered why.

"Of course," Elise said, "you *do* have a great house, but it wouldn't take much at all to divide it up into apartments. And you know the kind of rent those places bring."

Diana looked at her sharply. "Rent my house?" She said it in the same tone one might use to say, "Tear down Grace Cathedral?"

"Don't look so shocked. Some of the snootiest people I know are landlords. And maybe you don't need the income, but..."

"No, it's not that...." She tried to imagine strangers living in her house, sitting before her fireplace, walking up and down the staircase she and Mitch had painted, and she knew why she was hesitating over the job.

She looked at Elise, and she smiled weakly. "It's silly, I know. But... I thought this was home. I never expected to be moving again."

"Well," Elise said cheerfully, "that's what makes life an adventure, isn't it?"

"I'm not particularly big on adventures, either."

"Oh, yeah, right. Says the woman who'd seen more of this world by the time she was thirteen than most of us do in a lifetime."

"Which only means I see no point in doing it again." And she shrugged. "I'm thirty-one years old. I really don't think it was *too* farfetched of me to start to think about settling down."

"In the hotel business? Surely you jest."

"I suppose."

Elise leaned forward with the air of one inviting confidence. "Now," she insisted, "tell me about this great sex life of yours."

"Talking about me again, are you?"

Both women turned toward the door as Mitch sauntered in. His expression was easy, his bearing relaxed, but there was a watchfulness in his eyes that no one but Diana would have recognized. "'Morning, babe," he said. "Or should I say 'afternoon?

"I fixed your tire." He dropped a set of keys on her desk. "Thought you might need your car."

"Thank you." Diana's face was hot; her entire body was hot. And the knowing, slightly triumphant glint in Elise's eyes did nothing to ease her discomfort.

"Well," Elise said quickly, rising, "back to work. Congratulations again, Diana. We'll talk later."

Diana hardly knew when her assistant left the room. She felt trapped behind the small desk, wedged in by Mitch's nearness—by his size, his scent, by the gaze she couldn't quite meet. He didn't have to do anything; simple awareness of him sang through her nerves like an alternating current. The flood of memories left her weak. She had expected to handle this so much better. She had *planned* to handle it so much better.

"I usually make them breakfast," Mitch said quietly.

Diana picked up the car keys and stood, turning busily toward the file cabinet. Her breath came a little easier once her back was to him, but not much. "I don't have the first idea what you're talking about."

"My one-nighters." His voice was casual, even nonchalant, but his stance was alert. Beneath the surface was a hardness that made every muscle in Diana's body instinctively tense. "Some people say it's extravagant, but I like to think it shows a touch of class. Of course, you and I have always had different definitions for that word, haven't we?"

Diana found her purse in the file drawer and dropped the keys inside. She asked tightly, without turning around, "What do you want from me, Mitch?"

"Oh, I don't know. A good-morning kiss? A wake-up call? A 'thanks a lot and come again'? Or maybe you should have just left the money on the bed."

Diana slammed the drawer shut and whirled around. The heat that flared in her cheeks and glittered in her eyes was pure anger now, the kind of quick, hot temper that only he could evoke. "Fine, Mitch. Let's reduce this to its lowest denominator, shall we? I should have known it was too much to expect you to act like a gentleman even this once."

His eyes narrowed only slightly and his tone was easy and flip, but the stillness of his face was a window into the depths of his own anger. "A gentleman," he replied, "would have at least left a note on the pillow."

Diana tried to take a deep breath. It was difficult. "I have a lot on my mind, Mitch, and I don't have time to play games.'' The moment the words were out she knew how harsh they sounded. She hated herself for them, but she couldn't take them back. She couldn't take *anything* back. God, how could she be doing this so badly?

"Then I won't take much of your time. I just wondered if you would mind giving me a complete sexual history for the past—oh, three years or so. A guy can't be too careful these days, you—"

Diana lunged for him, her arm drawn back to strike. The rage was so intense, so swift and powerful and blinding, that she was not even aware of moving until he was upon her, his hand gripping her upraised arm with bruising force and holding it still. Diana stood there, her chest heaving, paralyzed with the impotency of rage and hurt and confusion, and most of it was directed at herself.

Mitch loomed over her, his eyes glinting with low furious sparks, his jaw tight beneath the light bristle of morning beard. The spasm that tightened her chest was only part hurt; the other part was pure, unadulterated longing. She hated him for that almost as much as she hated herself.

"You bastard."

"So we're even." He released her arm abruptly.

Diana turned away, drawing in a quick, unsteady breath. Why did it have to be like this between them? Why did it *always* have to be like this?

She waited until she could control her voice, if not her tumbling, tumultuous emotions, and she turned to face him. "What do you want from me, Mitch?" she demanded again, closing her fists at her sides. "Gratitude? Compliments on your performance? All right. The sex was good, the sex was great, sex is the only thing we ever did right together. But it meant *nothing*. Nothing has changed between us, and nothing ever will. You know that. So what do you want?"

He looked at her for a long steady moment. "I guess I wanted something to change. Hell, if I wanted to be treated like crap the morning after, I would've stayed married."

"Damn it, Mitch, will you stop this? Stop trying to pick a fight, stop trying to make me angry—"

"If making you mad is the only way I can get a re-action out of you, then damn right I'm going to pick a fight! We deserve more than this, Diana. Last night *meant* more than this."

The truth in his words, the challenge in his eyes, went through her like a knife, and Diana could not hold his gaze any longer. She swallowed hard to clear her throat but could not quite make her voice sound normal. "I know, Mitch. I . . ." And then she turned away, drawing a sharp breath. She tried to inject a light note into her voice but it came out sounding strident. "Well. You promised me regrets, and I certainly have them."

"No. You promised yourself regrets. You always were a great one for the self-fulfilling prophecy."

"Oh, for heaven's sake!" She turned back to him impatiently. "What are we fighting about, anyway? Because I had to go to work and you slept in? Really, Mitch, we used to be a great deal more creative than that!"

But he refused to be moved. His expression was taut, his tone sober. "Don't try it with me, Di. Just don't try it. You know damn good and well what this is about."

"Mitch, really—"

But when she tried to look away, he stepped in front of her, forcing her to meet his gaze. Not even two feet separated them, but the wall that stood between them was as thick as glacier ice and no physical proximity could melt it. "It's about waking up alone. It's about sneaking out while your lover sleeps and then pretending nothing ever happened—you used to do that, toward the end. Do you think I've forgotten that? Your way of drawing the line, calling the shots—of saying you'd share your body with me but not your soul. And all by yourself, princess, without thinking about it very hard at all, you managed to turn our marriage into a series of one-night stands. And I *hated* that."

"You didn't even notice!" she cried, as surprised by the memory as she was wounded by it—his and hers.

"How dare you accuse me of doing anything at all to our marriage when you barely even admitted we had one!"

"And don't think I didn't know why you were doing it, either," he interrupted grimly. "You wanted to punish me, and you did a better job than you'll ever know. Well, maybe I deserved it then, but last night— that wasn't fair, Diana."

She wanted to scream at him that she hadn't done anything, but she couldn't because he was right...right about what she had done, but not about why she had done it. He had never understood that. And now her head was spinning with hurt and confusion and loss and hope. Her breath was short and she couldn't have explained her reasons to him even if she had tried.

She hadn't been trying to punish him, merely to protect herself. And the odd thing—the sad and terrifying thing—was that even telling that now required more courage than she possessed.

So she met his gaze; she made her face perfectly expressionless, and she said, "I'm very busy here, Mitch."

When she started to turn away, he grabbed her arm, but only for the space of one sharp, furious breath. His eyes stormed for an instant with a hundred unspoken demands and accusations and then, in the next breath, the storm receded until his face was as expressionless as hers. A hint of weary bitterness in his smile was his only sign of emotion.

"You're one hell of a lady," he said, "and the sex is incredible, but I've got to tell you it's just not worth the hassle. Nobody's *that* good."

He turned and walked toward the door. There he looked back. "I parked your car on the street," he said. "You might want to move it before it's towed."

And that was it.

MITCH STARTED toward his room with every intention of packing his bags and checking out, and then he remembered he didn't have any bags to pack. Another time the irony would have at least drawn a wry smile; now it only made him want to hit something.

He didn't know why he was surprised. He didn't know what he had expected. And if he was angry with anyone at all, it was with himself. He had known how she would feel and what she would do; she had known how he would react. They were both so damn predictable. What would have happened if, just this once, he had given her what she needed instead of what she expected? If she had turned to him instead of away when she was confused?

Did it really matter? Maybe Diana was right; last night meant nothing. And maybe the only thing that bothered him was that she had been the first to say it.

He was standing by the front desk when Diana came out of her office, car keys in hand. She didn't glance in his direction, even though he was sure her awareness of him was just as keen as his was of her. Mitch couldn't help but notice the way people looked at her when she passed—the elegant woman with the sleekly knotted honey-gold hair, the flawless makeup and the smooth aristocratic features.... No matter how angry or hurt he was with her, Mitch never looked at her without feeling a surge of possessive pride mingled with yearning, and today the emotions twisted inside him like the slice of a knife. But he couldn't make himself look away.

"Mr. De—I mean, Mr. Mitchell."

Tim the bellman stood beside him, grinning a little at the near mistake over the name. As though it mattered. With an effort, Mitch dragged his gaze away from Diana. He even managed a smile. "Yeah, Tim. What's up?"

"It's been pretty busy," Tim admitted. "Checkout time and all. But I kept an eye on Miss Moore's car like you asked me. I caught a couple of kids fooling around once, but somebody else chased them off before I could."

Mitch nodded absently. Now he could see Diana through the glass door, moving down the steps toward the street. "Thanks, Tim."

The desk clerks were busy. Mitch decided a drink might be in order while he waited for the traffic to clear. Besides, he should at least take the time to decide where he was going.

He had started toward the Zephyr Room when suddenly he was struck by something. Harold. Where was he?

He turned back to Tim, who was moving toward the front doors with a luggage cart filled to capacity. Mitch caught up with him in a couple of strides. "Say, Tim, about those guys that were messing with the car—"

"They didn't do any damage," Tim assured him. "Probably just checking out the hubcaps."

"But the guy who chased them. Do you remember what he looked like?"

"Hard to say." Tim frowned. "Kind of a big guy. Plain looking."

"Hatchet face?" Mitch insisted, "Bad suit? Mid-forties, brown hair, brown shirt—"

Time's face cleared. "Yeah, that's him. Come to think of it, he might be a guest. I think I've seen him around in the last day or so."

Tim pushed the luggage cart through the door. Mitch went with him. He had parked against the curb at the corner of the hotel, a good fifty yards away. Diana had almost reached the car.

It could be nothing, he thought. *It's probably nothing.* And he called, "Hey, Di!"

She didn't hear him. He went down the steps, raising his voice. "Diana!"

She heard him that time. He could tell by the way her steps quickened. An urgency, crazy and inexplicable, was building in his chest, and he moved faster, threading his way through approaching guests and taxicab bumpers. "Diana, wait a minute! Listen to me!"

She had reached the car, and she paused before inserting the key into the lock to look up at him, scowling.

"Diana!" He began to run. "Don't get in the car! Wait!"

She put the key in the lock.

"Diana! Get away from the damn car!"

He launched himself at her. He remembered the astonishment on her face the moment before his body struck hers, he remembered her soft muffled cry. Then the world exploded in a roar of flames, and he remembered nothing else.

Chapter Nine

The roaring in Mitch's ears gradually faded; his vision cleared. But for the longest time it seemed he could hear nothing but the humming clutter of background noise, like a sound track run at high speed, and see nothing but a kaleidoscope of colors—purple, red, yellow, green. Slowly those colors separated into individual, vaguely familiar shapes...flowers. He was in a bed of pansies...*they* were in a bed of pansies. Diana's arms and legs were tangled up with his, and he could hear her coughing, feel her pushing against him.

"Di!" His voice sounded hoarse and faraway, and when he drew in a deep breath, the harsh fumes of the smoke-filled air stung his throat. He gripped her shoulders as he struggled to sit up. "Are you okay?"

She nodded, gasping, clinging to him. "Are you?"

The relief left him momentarily paralyzed and incapable of speech. In the background he heard the dim, distant wavering of sirens, voices shouting, flames crackling. One strand of hair had escaped Diana's perfect chignon; her eyes were an enormous midnight blue smudge in a parchment white face. But she was alive.

Mitch gained a sitting position, half supporting Diana and half leaning on her support. He drew another cautious deep breath, dimly amazed that he was able to do so. He straightened his legs, one at a time, and flexed his arms. "Yeah," he said, finally. "I'm okay."

Diana looked around dazedly, too stunned to feel the terror she surely should have felt, or to ask the questions to which she had every right to an answer. Huge plumes of dark smoke darkened the afternoon sky. Noxious gasoline fumes thickened the air, and the flames were so hot they felt like a sunburn against the back of her neck. People were running toward her, and she was sitting in the middle of a bed of crushed pansies, her stockings torn and her hair awry and one shoe missing.

She was in shock, she was quite sure. Something incredible had just happened here and it was entirely possible she might have died.... But somehow it didn't seem so incredible. Mitch had burst into her life a mere twenty-four hours ago and the world had just gone up in smoke and flames. What was surprising about that?

He helped her to stand. She held on tightly to his arm with one hand while she brushed the debris off her skirt, absently looking around for her shoe. And then she stopped and looked up.

Over Mitch's shoulder she could see the fireball that once had been her car. The flames were shooting so high that the limbs of a decorative elm on the other side of the street were singed, and Diana had to squint to look at it. She could have been inside that car.

Damn it all to hell, *Mitch* could have been inside that car.

She turned to him. "Are you sure you're okay?" she demanded hoarsely.

He nodded, breathing hard. "Yeah. I'm sure."

"Nothing broken?"

"No. Nothing."

"You're sure?"

"Yeah, honey, I'm sure. But you—"

"Good." Diana drew back her arm and struck him with all her might across the side of the face.

He staggered slightly, but Diana remained to catch only the briefest glimpse of the astonishment on his face. She turned sharply and, with all the dignity it was possible to display while wearing only one shoe and reeking of the flames that had almost killed them both, she limped away.

THE POLICE LEFT within the hour. Diana stopped shaking approximately an hour after that.

Mitch had presumably gone to the police station with the investigating officers. He would be comfortable there, in his milieu, surrounded by intrigue and high adventure, violence and drama. She hoped he enjoyed it. She hoped he relished it, reveled in it, played it for all it was worth and never, ever thought to involve her in one of his little schemes again.

"I really don't see how you can say this is his fault," Elise ventured. "I mean, he did save your life."

Diana's office had been a nonstop stream of people since someone had had the common sense to take her there when she staggered out of the bed of pansies. Finally, Diana had managed to get rid of everyone but Elise, who continued to circle like a protective mother bird, bringing Diana aspirin and wet cloths and glasses of ice water that she didn't need.

"My life wouldn't have been in danger if it hadn't been for him," Diana pointed out grimly.

But that wasn't the source of her anger, her shock, the tumult of emotions that had battered her raw inside. Mitch had been driving that car. It was Mitch they had tried to kill.

When she thought about the accusations he had flung at her earlier, she started to tremble all over again. How dare he criticize her for anything? How dare he even begin to ask for more of her when it took all her emotional energy just to protect herself from him, and had done so since the beginning?

The one thing Elise had brought her that she *did* need was a bottle of brandy from the bar, and she splashed a measure of it into a glass now. She had never taken a drink during working hours before in her life, but by her calculations she had been off duty since Arthur Hollings had officially told her to go home half an hour ago.

She leaned back in her chair and sipped the brandy. Her skirt had been brushed and sponged, her stockings changed, her face washed and her hair repinned. Except for the occasional slight tremor of her hand, no one, looking at her, would guess anything untoward had ever happened. And that was exactly the way she wanted it.

Elise gave a small shake of her head, perching on the edge of the chair near the door. "Well, I've got to say you're taking this well. Incredibly well. I mean, it's not every day a person gets her car blown up by assassins and misses being incinerated by a matter of seconds. No one would blame you if you made a semi-big deal out of it."

"I've had a lot of practice taking things well." Diana smiled thinly. "You forget, I was once married to the man."

"Do you mean—"

"No, to my knowledge this is the first time bomb-wielding assassins have been after him. But he did spend our wedding night in jail. I should have taken that as a warning.''

"In jail?'' echoed Elise. "For what?''

Diana sipped the brandy. "Some drunken cowboy said something rude to me and Mitch took it upon himself to teach him manners—with a pool cue. The charge was assault with a deadly weapon, I believe.''

Elise repressed a smile. "Well, at least he had a good reason.''

"Oh, Mitch always has a good reason.'' There was no humor in Diana's voice. "It's good unless you're the one who's sitting up at three o'clock in the morning imagining all the ways a body can be mangled on the highway, or trying to explain to your mother why a man answered your telephone with a string of expletives, or introducing a German prince to a man in boxer shorts and a T-shirt at a formal dinner party— when that man is your husband.''

This time it was a grin Elise repressed. "Sounds pretty exciting to me.''

"Oh, yes.'' Diana took a healthy swallow of the brandy, her tone flat. "It was definitely exciting.''

The brandy was, at long last, beginning to have a soporific effect, and it seemed to take Diana a few seconds longer than it should have to drag her thoughts back from the past. She looked at Elise. "I'm keeping you from your work. You don't have to stay with me.''

"Oh, yes, I do. I've volunteered to drive you home, which means I get the rest of the afternoon off. So anytime you're ready to go, just let me know."

Diana nodded. At the beginning of the weekend, the hotel was at less than sixty percent occupancy, and she knew there would be little, if anything, for either of them to do the rest of the day. But she wasn't ready to go home yet, either.

"I think I'll stay awhile," she said vaguely.

"Sure. But if you want to go home and go to bed, I'll be glad to tell Mitch where you are."

Diana shot her a warning look. "You do that on peril of our friendship."

"Diana," Elise said gently, "he's called six times. Don't you think you should at least talk to him? You know he's got to be worried."

Diana dismissed that with an impatient scowl. "The only thing he's worried about is whether I'm going to press charges."

Elise's eyes rounded. "You wouldn't, would you?"

Diana hesitated just long enough to generate a touch of real alarm in Elise's eyes, and then she sighed. "I suppose not. It would only be more trouble than it's worth, which is the way things usually are with Mitch."

There was a soft knock on the door and both women turned sharply toward it. Arthur Hollings poked his head around the corner.

"Ms. Moore," he said in some surprise. "I expected you would have gone home by now."

Diana was beginning to grow annoyed by the way people kept suggesting that.

Elise defended her. "She's not quite up to the ride yet, Mr. Hollings."

"Is there anything we can do? Shall I call back the doctor?"

"I'm fine," Diana said impatiently. "I'll leave in a little while." She lifted her glass to him. "I just wanted to finish my drink."

The slightest flicker of discomposure crossed his eyes, then was gone. "Yes, of course," he murmured. Then he added, "We merely wanted to thank you for diverting the press from the hotel. I needn't tell you how disastrous this kind of publicity could be, and in the midst of all you've been through, it showed genuine character to put the welfare of the hotel first. The sincerest admiration comes from Mr. Severenson as well as myself."

Diana sat up a little straighter, glancing at Elise, then looking back to Arthur Hollings. "I would have done it if I'd had the chance," she said, "but no one from the press has even approached me."

Arthur looked only slightly surprised. Clearly he did not care who had saved the hotel from unflattering publicity, as long as it had been done, and Diana couldn't blame him for that.

"Well," he said, "I suppose Mr. DeSalvo must have done it, then. I must remember to thank him. Right now—" he glanced at his watch "—I have a dinner meeting outside the hotel that simply can't be postponed. Good night, ladies." He turned back. "Oh, and Ms. Moore, sympathies again on your ordeal. Shall we expect you in the morning?"

"I'll be here."

He nodded once, as though he had expected no other reply, and closed the door behind him.

Elise gave a small incredulous shake of her head. "Do you believe that guy? You're almost blown to smithereens right before his eyes, and all he wants to know is if you'll be in tomorrow? Wouldn't you think he'd at least be curious about who and what and how—or even a little impressed? I'd settle for impressed. I mean, how many cars do you think *he's* seen bombed in his lifetime?"

Diana smiled absently. "He's only doing his job. Besides, I'd be willing to lay a wager that he already knows the who and what and how. Or at least, more than we do."

But she was thinking about what he had said with a mixture of guilt and curiosity. She must have been more deeply upset than she had yet to accept, because the possible damage to the reputation of the hotel had not been her first thought. She supposed in the back of her mind she had noticed the absence of the press, and she might even have remarked on the perfunctory nature of the police interview, but she had simply assumed someone else had taken care of it. If that someone was Mitch... It wasn't like him. Not at all.

"It's almost six," Elise said. "I'll bet I could get a television set in here in time for the news."

Diana looked at her for a moment thoughtfully. "You may have just defined the essential trouble with my ex-husband. It's virtually impossible to be around him for more than a few days at a time without ending up on the evening news. And that's another thing I should have known from the beginning."

Then she sighed, leaned back in her chair and poured more brandy. "All right," she agreed, resigned. "Bring in the television."

IT WAS ALMOST DARK by the time Mitch left the police station. It took him another twenty minutes to fight his way through the crush of reporters and cameras— although the truth was, he didn't do a whole lot of fighting. He was a born publicity hound and generally enjoyed everything about being in the spotlight, even when it was something like this that put him there. If there had been no one but himself involved, he would have played it to the hilt—particularly since the perpetrators were now safely behind bars, ready to confess to everything from fixing parking tickets to kidnapping Judge Crater. But he had more than himself to think of now, and when he manipulated the press it was for Diana's sake, not his own.

Every time he thought about how close she had come, he broke out in a cold sweat, and the surge of anger turned his muscles to steel. He had almost lost her. *He had almost lost her.*

Mitch walked along the street and turned the corner. The footfalls behind him matched his pace, but when Mitch stopped without warning, they did not have time to slow. Mitch spun around, caught the lapels of the man's jacket in both hands and slammed him up against the wall.

"All right, Harold," he demanded in a low voice, breathing hard. "Talk."

In the distorting glow of a distant streetlight, the other man's face looked slack with shock. "I don't know what—"

Mitch drew back and slammed him against the wall again, this time pinning him there with the heel of his hand against the man's throat. "Where were you, you son of a bitch? You've been dogging my steps since I got off the plane yesterday, so where the hell were you when those bastards were planting a bomb on my wife's car? Were you out there helping them? *Were you?*"

Harold grabbed Mitch's wrist and succeeded in easing the pressure on his throat just enough to allow a few desperate gasps for air. "Are you crazy?" he wheezed. "Who the hell do you think was chasing those punks down for the cops? Let me go, damn it!"

Mitch looked at him for another long moment, then cautiously stepped back. Harold flung his hand away and bent over at the waist, coughing and gasping for breath. "They were right!" he managed at last. "You're a lunatic!"

Mitch looked at him thoughtfully. "Who was right?"

Harold did not answer.

After a moment, Mitch took out a cigarette and tapped it against the back of his hand. "It was plastique," he said. "And a time-delay trip wire. Ten seconds after the door was opened, just about the time the driver was putting on his seat belt—kablooey. It has a kind of crude sophistication to it you can't help but admire."

Harold cast him a dry look, bringing his breathing slowly under control. "They didn't have a lot of time for subtlety," he pointed out. "If you had parked in a garage like a normal person, they could have come up with something a lot more high-tech."

"Well, at least I did something right," Mitch muttered. He stuck the cigarette in his mouth. "You got a match?"

Harold just glared at him.

With a small gesture of his hand, Mitch started back the way he had come. After a moment, Harold fell rather grudgingly into step beside him.

"So," Mitch said. "Do you think this is it?"

"Probably. As quick as those guys went belly-up, I'd say their West Coast connections aren't very strong. Besides..." He slanted a glance at Mitch. "They've made their point, don't you think?"

"I hope to God so."

He glanced at Harold. "I guess this is it for you, huh? Off the payroll?"

"Not until I make my final report."

"Bet there's a bonus in it for you. Who're you working for, anyway?"

Harold hesitated a moment, then said, "Your publisher."

It took Mitch a beat to absorb that, and then he burst into laughter. "The sharks don't miss a trick when it comes to the golden goose, do they? Not that I'm complaining. Don't count on that bonus, by the way," he added. "Those guys can squeeze a nickel 'til the eagle screams. Matter of fact, you probably should've asked for cash up front."

He grinned and draped an arm around the other man's shoulders. Harold looked surprised and uncomfortable. "Sorry about earlier," Mitch said. "How about giving me a lift? I didn't exactly bring my car."

Harold hesitated, obviously debating with himself. Then he grinned, gave a shake of his head and said, "Ah, hell. Why not?"

Chapter Ten

"The owner of the car, described as an acquaintance of Mr. DeSalvo's, was not present. No one was injured in the blast, and two suspects are now being held for questioning in connection with the incident." The blond anchorwoman turned on cue to face another camera. "In Washington tonight . . ."

Diana shook her head in dim amazement as Elise got up and turned the television off. "How does he do it?" she murmured. "There must have been a dozen witnesses who knew who I was. The *police* knew who I was. He even managed to get them to point their cameras toward the candy shop across the street instead of at the hotel."

"Well, I'm not entirely sure I'd appreciate being referred to as an acquaintance if it had been my car that had been blown up." Elise's tone was slightly disgruntled. "I mean, what was he doing driving an 'acquaintance's' car, anyway? It makes you sound like someone he just picked up at a bar or something.''

Diana chuckled softly. The sound surprised her almost as much as it did Elise. "Yes, it does, doesn't it?'' She shrugged. "Of course, Mitch always did see the truth as something he could manipulate to fit the story line. That's the fiction writer in him, I suppose. I never thought I'd see the day that would come in handy.''

Elise regarded her thoughtfully. "You really are crazy about him, aren't you?''

Diana stared at her friend. It was a moment before she could speak. "The man came storming in here, turned my hotel into a circus, blew up my car and very nearly got me killed. Would you like to explain to me please just exactly what it is I've done or said that makes you think I'm crazy about him?''

Elise smiled in a maddening way. "Just a hunch.''

Diana knew that Elise was only teasing her to take her mind off recent events, but she was in no mood to take it in good humor. Not that the subject of Mitch was ever one she had been inclined to take lightly. "Your hunches could use some work," she said shortly.

Elise's voice was thoughtful as she asked, "What in the world happened to you guys, anyway?''

Diana took a sip of the brandy. "You can't be serious. What *didn't* happen to us?''

"Yeah, but there must have been something specific. Marriages don't just end for no reason."

"That's the hell of it, you know." Diana tried to keep her voice nonchalant. "There were reasons, dozens of them. But there was never any one moment, one specific thing that I could point to and say, 'There, this is it. This is what killed my marriage.'" She shrugged. "Sometimes I think it was exhaustion, more than anything else, that led to the divorce. We were both just too tired to fight anymore. On the other hand, it was never exactly what you'd call a match made in heaven."

"You knew that when you married him," Elise pointed out.

Diana's frown was thoughtful as she stared into the golden liquid. "I married him," she said, "because he took me to places I'd never been before, and I thought I'd seen everything. Just knowing him was an adventure. He was the brashest, most exciting, most *different* man I'd ever known, and that's why I married him. That's also why I couldn't live with him."

The sharp buzz of the telephone snatched Diana back from the edge of becoming maudlin, and she was a little embarrassed to see how close she had come. She reached for the telephone, but Elise was closer and stayed her hand.

"It's probably for me, anyway," she said. "You're not supposed to be here, remember?"

She spoke into the receiver for only a few seconds, ending with "Thanks, Carla."

When she hung up, Diana said, "Look, I don't need a baby-sitter. Go take care of your job."

"I asked Carla to buzz me when Mitch got back to the hotel," she answered. And at Diana's look she added defensively, "Hey, the two of you almost got blown up together. I thought you'd want to know when he got back safe and sound. He's in the Zephyr Room."

"I don't want to know where he is," Diana said tersely. "I don't ever want to see him again, in or out of this hotel."

She recalled she had said something similar that fateful day they had decided—by mutual consent and at full pitch—that divorce was the only way to save their sanity. It hadn't worked then, and she had no fear that it would work now. Mitch was one of those things in life, like a bad debt or an ill-fitting pair of shoes, that just kept turning up at the most inconvenient times, a mocking reminder of past mistakes. It had always been that way and always would be, and her wishing it were different would not make it so.

Elise smiled. "If I thought you really meant that, I *would* feel sorry for you. You realize of course that you are on the verge of turning away what just might possibly be the last real man in America?"

Diana started to form a sarcastic protest, then changed her mind. "I know. And that's what attracted me to him in the first place, I suppose. What else could it have been? It certainly wasn't his dime-store wardrobe or barroom manners or that oh-so-charming way he has of sweeping a woman off her feet—literally."

Despite the harsh words, Diana had to fight back a reminiscent, almost tender smile, and after a moment she admitted, "Or maybe it was all those things. It's odd, isn't it, how wanting is almost always so much more exciting than having? Perhaps he was a little too real for me. Or perhaps—" she took a final sip of the brandy "—I was too much of a woman for him."

Elise grinned. "Now you're talking. But you know something?" Her tone gentled a fraction. "You really should be talking to him, not me."

Diana's smile was bitter. "Mitch and I don't talk. We shout. We fence. We take cheap shots, we push each other's buttons, we make each other crazy, but we never, ever talk."

Elise shook her head. "I know it's none of my business. I know you think I'm being a real pest on the subject. But I like you, honey. And Mitch—well, you've got to admit he's every woman's fantasy. The two of you together could be like some kind of fairy tale. I just hate to see you screw up your chances."

"Wait a minute." Diana's eyes widened. "Are you and I still in the same conversation? Mitch DeSalvo, every woman's fantasy? Okay, so he might have a certain crude sex appeal—very crude—but he's hardly pin-up material. He's a cheap paperback writer, for heaven's sake, with no ambition whatsoever to be anything more. He eats potato chips in bed and leaves open beer cans around until they start growing mold. His idea of classical music is Willie Nelson and he reads the supermarket tabloids to keep up with current events! This is every woman's fantasy?"

"The man every woman wants to tame," agreed Elise. "You had your chance, and you blew it."

Diana was a little startled. Was that what it was, then? Had she wanted him only to tame him, to remake him and then keep him like a saddle-broken stallion, to show off to her friends? If so, it was no wonder Mitch had left her.

She started to lift the empty glass, then swallowed hard. "Some men are just untamable," she said. "I guess I should have realized from the first he was one of them. That was my mistake."

"We're all entitled to one, I guess," Elise responded cheerfully. And though her next words were casual, the look she slid toward Diana was decidedly odd. "Just so *I* don't make a mistake...are you sure? I mean, what you said about your never wanting to see Mitch again—you meant it?"

Something made Diana hesitate.

"Because you guys have been hanging on to this thing for years. Sooner or later you're going to have to stop talking about it and call it quits once and for all."

"We're divorced," Diana interjected. "How much more 'quits' can you get?"

"You know what I mean," Elise replied placidly. "All I'm saying is that if this is the time you decide to get serious, I wish you'd let me know because there are a lot of women who find your ex-husband very attractive. And I happen to be one of them."

Diana was stunned, and for a long moment all she could do was stare at Elise. She didn't know what shocked her most: Elise's frank confession or the stab of betrayal and, yes, jealousy that went through her with the words. She and Mitch were divorced. She had no claim on him. Only moments ago she had told Elise she never wanted to see him again and she had meant it. She had no right to feel anything where Mitch was concerned. If anything, she should be grateful that someone else was offering to divert his attention from her. But grateful was the last thing she felt.

She was saved from the necessity of a response by the ringing of the telephone. She reached for it quickly. It might be Mitch.

"Thank God."

The voice on the other end of the line was masculine, faintly accented and oddly familiar. But because it wasn't Mitch, Diana had a moment's trouble placing the voice.

"It wasn't your car," he went on. "I thought it must have been, and when I called you at home and got no answer... Well, I shouldn't like to relive these last few moments, I must say. Darling, you are all right?"

"Etienne," Diana managed at last in a somewhat strangled tone. "I—for heaven's sake, how did you—?"

"You made the national news. Your Mr. DeSalvo is something of a celebrity, and car bombings are not an ordinary occurrence, even in San Francisco. When I saw the hotel in the background and heard reports of this mysterious woman..." His voice abruptly changed. "It *was* you, wasn't it?" he demanded. "It was your car some maniac blew to the heavens, wasn't it?"

Diana replied uncomfortably, "Etienne, you make it sound so much worse than it was."

"I wasn't aware that it was possible to underestimate the horror of a terrorist attack."

"It wasn't a terrorist attack. It was—"

"My God, Diana, were you hurt? Why didn't you call me?"

"Etienne, I—"

"Never mind, I've already reserved a flight. It leaves in an hour and I can be there by—"

"No, don't." Her voice was sharper than she intended, and the intensity vibrated across the line, leaving a startled and empty silence. "Don't come here."

That was all she said, but behind the words was so much more. *Don't come here. I don't need you. I don't want you. You're not Mitch.*

It's over.

As clearly as if it had been spoken out loud, the truth reverberated between them. And the worst was, until that moment Diana had not even known what the truth was, not really. For all these months she had believed something wonderful was possible with Etienne, but now... there was Mitch.

After what seemed a long time Etienne spoke. His voice sounded farther than a mere continent away, distant and removed. "Of course. If you think it's best."

There was a lump in her throat, and for a moment she couldn't reply. She was aware of Elise's unabashed attention in the background. "I—I do."

"I see."

There was another brief and painful silence. Then Etienne added, "I should mention that it looks as though my business will keep me here longer than I'd planned. Perhaps another week."

"Call me." Diana didn't know what to say. "I'd like to know—when you get in."

"Yes." Perhaps a touch of sarcasm. "We'll have lunch."

"Etienne, I'm sorry...that I worried you."

"I'm glad you're all right, Diana." Another long pause. Goodbye waiting to be said. "Good night."

"Thank you—for calling."

And that was it. He disconnected. In a moment, so did Diana.

She took an unsteady breath. "Why do I have the feeling I could have handled that so much better?"

Elise gave her a sympathetic smile. "It's been a long day."

She got up and crossed to the coatrack, removing Diana's coat. "Come on, I'll drive you home. If we hang around here much longer, I'm going to get stuck in traffic on the way back."

Diana focused on the turn of the conversation with difficulty. "I thought you said you had the rest of the day off."

"I do." Elise's back was to her, masking her expression as she brushed a wrinkle from the coat. "But I figured as long as Mitch is alone in the bar—and since you're not interested in keeping him company— maybe I would."

She smiled as she handed Diana her coat. Diana took it as she got slowly to her feet. Then she walked back to the coatrack and replaced it on the hook.

The odd thing was, she truly had no idea what she was going to say until she spoke. "I'll tell you what, Elise." Her voice was casual and easy. "You go on home. I think I'll stay."

"But—"

"No, I insist." She turned to Elise and said deliberately, "I'm going to stop by the bar and have another drink. I may be awhile. I'll call a cab when I'm ready to leave."

Elise looked reluctant. "If you're sure..."

"I am."

"I could wait."

"Not necessary," Diana assured her as she opened the door.

"All right. If you're sure."

And though the voice sounded unhappy, Diana was almost certain she saw a self-satisfied smile touch her friend's lips just before she left the room. But by the time it struck Diana that she had been manipulated, it was too late to turn back. And she was not at all sure she wanted to.

"...ALTHOUGH DETAILS remain sketchy at this hour, we can be assured of further developments in this case, which already is beginning to bear a strong resemblance to a Sal Mitchell novel. Back to you in the studio, Jeff.''

Mitch smothered a moan as the camera shot switched from the good-looking reporter strategically posed in front of the blackened car to the good-looking reporter posed at the studio anchor desk. That was the third time in the past half hour he had been forced to relive the drama via the miracle of television.

"It's enough to put a man off his nachos for a week,'' he muttered, and pushed the plate away.

He and Harold had taken seats at the darkened end of the bar. Jon the bartender seemed to have a morbid fascination with the entire episode—or perhaps he thought he was doing Mitch a favor—and he kept flipping through the channels searching for news.

Mitch raised his voice a little to get Jon's attention. "Isn't it time for the floor show?''

"Sorry.'' Jon gave an abashed grin and turned off the television set. "I guess the whole thing doesn't fascinate you as much as it does the rest of us. But you've got to understand this is the most excitement this old place has seen since . . .'' His grin widened as he concluded, "Well, since the riot in the lobby yesterday when you arrived. There seems to be a pattern developing here.''

Mitch sipped his beer, muttering, "Yeah, tell me about it.''

"Anything else I can get for you?"

"Just keep the beers coming. And Jon—" he lifted an admonishing finger "—low profile, okay?"

Jon responded with a sober face and a hand raised in the Boy Scout salute. "On my honor."

Mitch figured, considering all the people he had sworn to secrecy, he had about three hours before the press descended on him—and Diana—en masse.

"I'll tell you one thing, Harold," he said. "I sure know how to make an impression."

Harold dedicated himself to his own plate of nachos and did not reply.

"That's what I've been trying to do, you know, since the first minute I met her," Mitch continued. "The trouble is, I keep making the wrong kind of impression."

Mitch gazed into his beer thoughtfully for a moment.

"No," he decided, and lifted the mug again. "The real trouble is, I don't know *why* I wanted her to be impressed in the first place. I never have been able to figure that one out."

He drained the mug and slid it across the bar for a refill. His voice grew reminiscent. "I remember the first time I met her. My editor was in town and I came over to meet him for dinner. There she was, so crisp and efficient and bossing everybody around, and it was like somebody socked me in the throat. It was like everything just stopped in its tracks for a split second and this big neon sign started flashing *Here she is. This is the one.* Is that crazy, or what? The last thing I was looking for was a woman to get serious about. And if I had been, it wouldn't have been her. She wasn't even my type."

Jon placed another mug of beer before him. "I never could figure that out. How could I get knocked right out of the ballpark by a woman I didn't even like?"

He shook out a cigarette and tapped it absently on the bar. "She was wearing a white silk suit, kind of clingy and shimmery, and her hair in one of those schoolteacher twists. I'd never seen hair just that color before, just that combination of gold and brown. Every once in a while I'll try to describe it, you know, to give a character in one of my books hair like that, but—hell, you've seen her. What would you call it?"

Harold didn't answer, and Mitch nodded sagely. "See. They haven't invented the color yet." He stuck the cigarette casually in his mouth and patted his pockets for a match. "I'll bet you didn't know that the word 'orange' wasn't in the English language until explorers came to the tropics and discovered orange trees. There wasn't even such a color. Seems hard to imagine, doesn't it?"

This time Harold grunted.

"Anyway..." Mitch reached for the book of matches and ashtray at the next stool. "She was some looker, I won't deny that. Classy? You bet. And smart—hell, she could run this hotel if she had a mind to. I've never met anybody in my life who was more sure of herself, together, completely fearless."

Mitch touched a match to the tip of the cigarette.

"She made me crazy." He observed the cigarette thoughtfully. "I'm talking locoweed crazy. I've always thought of myself as a pretty even-tempered guy, but she could make me madder faster than anybody I've ever known. And when *she* got mad..." He gave a small shake of his head and lifted his beer mug. "Let's just say a smart man would try his damnedest not to be in the same county with her when she got mad. And if I had one talent, it was for making her mad."

He took another long swallow of his beer. "So why, you ask, did I ever get myself tangled up with a she-devil like that? Well, for one thing, she's a hell of a sexy woman. Those eyes, that hair...great figure. Legs that go all the way up to her armpits, thighs like an ice skater. And there's this thing she does with her tongue...."

Harold glanced at him uneasily. "Hey, man, I don't think you should be telling me this."

"Just wanted to see if I had your attention. But you're right," Mitch added mildly, lifting his mug.

"And if I ever hear you repeating what I just said to anybody, I'm afraid I'll have to kill you."

He drank from his mug. "Two things a man should never do while drinking," he said contemplatively, tapping ashes from his cigarette. "Operate motorized vehicles, and talk about his wife." His tone dropped a fraction as he corrected, "*Ex*-wife."

"Listen, Mr. DeSalvo..."

"Call me Mitch. We've been through life and death together, and if that doesn't put us on a first-name basis, I don't know what will."

"Whatever." Harold looked a little uncomfortable. "Listen, you can say this is none of my business—hell, it's not—but it doesn't take a radio head-doctor to see you've still got it bad for your ex. So why are you sitting in a bar spilling your guts to a stranger when you could be hashing it out with her?"

"Haven't you noticed? The lady isn't taking my calls. Not that it matters. I wouldn't know what to say to her if she did."

"Come on, a guy like you? All those books you write? How can you not know what to say? I bet you're just like that guy Spindler you write about. Now there's one smooth-talking dude. And you never see him going without on a cold winter's night, do you?"

Mitch smiled a little, flattered as always to know someone was out there reading his books. "Yeah, well if I could live like Spindler, I guess I wouldn't have to write about him."

Harold grunted thoughtfully. "On second thought, after this afternoon, I'm not so sure I'd want your life—or Spindler's, either, you want to know the truth."

"Diana always called me a magnet for trouble," Mitch said. "She was right, of course. But hell, a few bar fights, a run-in with a cop in a bad mood now and then, a couple of dollars over the limit on the wrong horse—that's not trouble, that's just the price of living. She knew she wasn't marrying Mr. Suburbia. She knew what kind of guy I was. What she called trouble I called the spice that kept life interesting . . . until today." He drew deeply on the cigarette and exhaled a long stream of smoke. His voice was quiet as he finished. "Now it doesn't seem so interesting anymore."

Harold said nothing.

Mitch stared at his cigarette with an expression of rueful contempt. "She was right about something else," he said. "I've got absolutely no character."

He ground the cigarette out in the ashtray until nothing remained but a shredded filter.

"I really blew it this time, Harold," he said softly. "Damned if I didn't."

Mitch pushed himself up from the bar and dug into his pocket for some bills. "Listen, Harold. Take the rest of the night off. I'm going to go up and see what kind of flight I can get out of here."

Harold looked surprised. "You're leaving?"

"No point in hanging around any longer. Looks like I've done just about all the damage I can do."

"Where are you going?"

Mitch shrugged.

Harold started to rise. "I've got to clear this with my superiors."

Mitch waved him back onto the stool. "Finish your beer. I'll clear it with your superiors." He hesitated. "Come to think of it, I am your superior. So have another beer. Have two."

Harold grinned and gave a shake of his head. "You're really a character, aren't you? And to think I didn't believe half of what they said about you."

"Well, now you know better." Mitch turned to go.

"You're not going to talk to her?"

Mitch stopped, and shook his head. "Nothing to say. Except..." He drew a long breath. His next words were so low they were almost inaudible. "I'm so damn sorry."

Harold looked at him soberly. "That'd be a start."

Mitch said nothing for a long time. Then he turned back toward the exit. "Been nice knowing you, Harold. Have a good life."

Chapter Eleven

When the bartender told Diana that Mitch had gone to his room, she almost let it go at that. What did she have to say to him, after all? What could either of them possibly say?

Nonetheless, she found herself standing outside the Oleander Suite, her throat dry, her palms sweating. She suddenly knew what she wanted to say to him. The question was whether or not she had the courage.

In the few seconds it took him to answer her knock, she almost changed her mind. She had half turned toward the elevators when he opened the door.

In that first instant, there was no disguising the surprise and welcome in his eyes; without it Diana might not have stayed. But almost before she could blink, the smooth mask was back again and he stepped away from the door, gesturing her inside with an elaborate wave of his arm.

"Don't tell me. You came to thank me. No need, really. I would have done the same for any female about to set off a bomb."

"Thank you?" Diana snapped. "I ought to press charges."

She stepped inside. This was easy, this was familiar: the quick sharp banter, thrust and parry, advance and retreat. She could deal with this.

"Fickle, thy name is Woman." He closed the door behind her.

That was when Diana noticed the canvas duffel bag on the sofa. It wasn't much, but it was one of the unmistakable signs of packing.

He was leaving. Again.

He noticed the direction of her gaze and the tension between them was palpable. For a moment, neither of them spoke.

Then Diana said, ignoring the redundancy, "You're leaving?" Her tone was flat, so that it was more of a statement than a question.

He crossed the room easily toward the bag. "You know me, babe. Never one to overstay my welcome."

"So just when exactly would you say your welcome ended?" she demanded. "With the riot you started in the lobby or the party you crashed or the firebomb?"

"Good point." He slid open the door of the writing desk and helped himself to the supply of stationery and pens.

"For heaven's sake, Mitch—"

"Hey, I'm paying for it." He unzipped the bag and dumped the stationery inside.

"We're billing you for those towels."

"Give me a break. I'm trying to furnish an apartment."

"Do you have any idea how much those ashtrays cost us?"

"No, but I'm sure you can tell me. To the penny."

"You are without a doubt the biggest sleaze who ever walked the face of the earth."

"Yeah, I know." He grinned at her over his shoulder as he rezipped the bag. "But admit it. You're going to miss the hell out of me."

The words went through her like a knife. Miss him? *Miss him?* Every hour of every day for the past three years she had missed him. Missing him was a way of life, a habit, like putting sugar in her coffee or brushing her teeth. He was here and her life was a circus, bright colors and rushing winds; he went away and there it was again—missing him, the one thing at which she had become an expert.

"So that's it, Mitch?" Her voice was icy with anger. "You burst in here, turn my life upside down, almost get me killed, and then you just *leave?*"

His smile seemed a little weak. "Well, you know what they say. My job here is finished."

"You weren't even going to *tell* me?"

The last signs of humor faded, and he looked tired from maintaining the effort. "I left a message on your home machine. I—"

"You left a message on the machine!" Words momentarily failed her. She drew a sharp breath and turned her back on him, struggling for composure.

"Well, I've got to hand it to you, Mitch," she finally managed. "That took nerve, even for you."

"Yeah, well, I didn't want to leave without saying goodbye."

It could have been just another one of his flip comments, another parting shot on the way out the door...but it wasn't. His tone was too quiet, his words too controlled, and somehow Diana just knew. She had known from the moment she had walked into the room.

She turned around to look at him.

There was a split second when he looked into her eyes that Mitch almost lost his resolve. He looked into those eyes and nothing else mattered, nothing else made sense, except that he keep looking into those eyes forever... which was exactly the way he had felt the first time he'd seen her. He was paying the price now for thinking with his hormones then; he wasn't going to let it happen again.

He drew a breath, thrusting his fingers through his hair. "Wow," he said. "This is weird. We've never said it before, do you realize that? Even when you kicked me out.''

Diana's heart was beating hard. "I didn't kick you out. You left."

But he was not distracted. He looked at her steadily, sadly. "We never said goodbye."

"I suppose..." Diana swallowed hard. "...that's always been part of the problem."

"I guess."

Mitch tried to look away from her and he couldn't. *So close,* he thought. Another thirty seconds and he would have made a clean escape, none of this would be happening. He wouldn't be standing here with silence ringing between them, trying to find some way to say goodbye—after three long and painful years—to the only woman he had ever loved.

Diana saved him the trouble. She always had, if he stalled about something long enough.

"So," she said. There was a trace of hesitance in her voice, even a hint of disbelief, but her expression was calm and accepting. "This is it, then."

Mitch tried to take another deep breath and found he couldn't. "Yeah," he said. "Looks like it."

Somehow he managed a smile. It hurt his face. "You always did say someday I'd go too far. Well, damned if I didn't."

He couldn't hold the smile any longer, or the light tone. "You were right, Di. We've never been anything but trouble to each other. I don't know why it took an explosion to make me see that."

"Well." Diana's voice sounded a little thick. "Subtlety was never your strong suit."

He looked at her with nothing but naked pain on his face. "I wouldn't have hurt you for anything in the world, honey, you know that. But every time I'm around you, one of us ends up getting hurt. I just— don't think, sometimes. But you know that. You know me better than anybody."

Yes, she thought, and for a moment she was afraid the lump in her throat would choke off her breath. *Just like you know me. And that's why we can do this to each other, tear each other's hearts out with our bare hands without even leaving a mark....*

"We're like—bad chemicals, Mitch. You mix the wrong things together and something explosive is bound to happen. It's a law of nature."

His expression softened for a moment, and a stab of yearning went right through her soul.

"Yeah," he said. "There always were a lot of fireworks, weren't there?"

Diana swallowed hard. "Where are you going?"

She could not believe how calm her voice sounded, how resigned. That was not what she wanted to say. None of this was what she had come here to say and every time a sentence escaped her lips, she was shocked, because it was as though someone else had spoken.

Why are you doing this? I want you to come home with me. I want you to come home and stay. I want to hold you there and keep you safe. And you'll stay with me, damn it, Mitch. You'll never leave me again.... That was what she had come here to say.

But of course she couldn't.

"I don't know," Mitch said. "I kind of had this idea, now that things have opened up in eastern Europe.... I've always wanted to see Moscow."

Diana tried to prevent a wave of wifely anxiety as visions of assassins and spies assailed her. She wasn't a wife anymore; it wasn't her place to worry about him—at home or abroad.

She smiled stiffly. "Ian Fleming, eat your heart out."

"Right."

Mitch knew that he was stalling for time, looking for things to say, ways to keep her in the room. He found himself thinking about lasts. The last time he'd ever see her smile like that, when she didn't really mean it but was trying to ease the tension. The last time he'd ever watch her lift her hand to smooth back that errant strand of hair that was usually in her imagination. The last time he'd smell the cool exotic scent of her perfume, stand close enough to embrace her...

They had already had so many lasts, maybe all they were allowed. How much longer could he postpone the end?

Let it go, Mitch. Let her go. It's time.

"So what about you?" he asked. "I hope I didn't get you into any trouble with your boss, and if you want me to talk to him..."

"Actually..." Diana clasped her hands tightly before her. "I got a job offer. In New Orleans. So it looks as though I'll be leaving, too."

Another surprise. The last thing on her mind had been that job offer, and certainly she had not planned on telling Mitch about it. And until she spoke the words, she was not aware of having made a decision about the job. But suddenly it all made sense. And she knew the decision had been made for her long ago.

Mitch stared at her. "New Orleans? But I thought you liked it here."

"I like New Orleans, too."

Mitch did not know why that statement should make him feel so betrayed. Why thinking of San Francisco without Diana was like thinking of nothing at all. Why thinking of her away from the place where he had known her and loved her and lived with her left him feeling so bereft.

"What about the house?" It was an effort to keep his voice even.

She avoided his eyes. "I haven't decided yet. It's all come up so sud—"

The floor began to rumble, the walls to shake. The tremor was stronger than the one the day before, powerful enough to dislodge a vase from a high shelf on the wall behind Mitch. Diana saw it start to fall and she lurched toward it, but the floor actually seemed to pitch; she was thrown off balance and into Mitch's arms. The vase crashed on the floor, along with a half-empty glass of whiskey and a table lamp, then everything was still. It was over almost before Diana could register alarm.

All she really registered was the strength of Mitch's arms, the heat of his chest, his breath against her cheek. When her heart began to pound, she was not certain whether it was the residual effects of the tremor, or the simple, inescapable power of Mitch's nearness. The awareness of him, the need of him, the magnetism of him.... Would she ever get over it? Was she foolish to even try?

For a long moment they didn't move. Diana had fallen against him sideways and he had caught her with one arm around her shoulders, the other steadying her waist. Her hand was braced against his forearm. She looked up at him; he held her gaze. She thought, *Mitch, please* . . .

But she didn't know how she would have finished the sentence if she had been given the chance.

He released her slowly. "That was a good one," he said. He took a breath. "I'll never get used to it. But it doesn't bother you a bit, does it?"

In the background Diana heard disturbances in the hall—doors slamming, querulous and demanding voices. She squared her shoulders as she stepped away from Mitch's embrace, brushing at a spot of plaster dust on her jacket. "I spent three years in Japan, remember? There's a place that knows something about earthquakes."

Another door slammed in the hall. Diana glanced in that direction. "Sounds like some of the guests are upset. I'd better see what I can do."

"I'll walk out with you." Mitch crossed to the sofa and picked up his duffel bag, righting the lamp on his way.

Diana swallowed hard. "So you're leaving now, tonight?"

He shrugged. "No reason to hang around, is there?"

No reason to hang around.... That, she supposed, summed up their relationship from start to finish. If only they had both accepted it sooner.

"No."

She turned toward the door, then looked back. She smiled slightly.

"That's funny," she said. "There was a tremor yesterday when you arrived, and another one now, when you're leaving. Symbolic, somehow, don't you think?''

Mitch swallowed his disappointment. He didn't even know what he was disappointed about.

"Yeah, well, I always did like to make an impression.''

He gestured her to precede him toward the door. Her hand was on the doorknob and he was one step behind her when she turned to look at him. "Mitch..."

It hit with a force of a freight train. No slow rumbling and shaking this time, but a roaring, thunderous quake that started out strong and only grew stronger. The light fixture overhead swung wildly on its chain. A rain of plaster poured from the ceiling. Diana held on to the doorknob with both hands to keep her balance. She thought she cried out but she couldn't tell; she couldn't even hear her own voice. That was the first two seconds.

Mitch lurched toward her, his face a blur of shock and urgency. He shouted something that she couldn't hear; his weight knocked her back against the door and pinned her there. The lamp shattered. A glass-topped table tipped and crashed. Pictures flew from the walls. There was a sharp snapping sound over their heads and an ominous crack appeared above the doorjamb. Mitch grabbed her hand and shouted again; she could not hear the words but she knew what he meant. Ducking low, shielding their heads as best they could from falling debris, they began to half stumble, half crawl toward the shelter of the big writing desk across the room. That was the next four seconds.

They flung themselves beneath the desk just as a tall mahogany armoire that concealed the television and VCR crashed to the floor in a cloud of smoke. The corner of it caught the arm of the sofa and tipped the heavy piece of furniture over backward. A small chair splintered with its weight.

Diana might have screamed then. She thought surely she did; how could anyone endure such horror, such noise, such violent, relentless destruction and not scream and scream at the top of her lungs until she had no breath? But if she screamed, she didn't know it, because her face was pressed into Mitch's shoulder in the small space, her eyes tightly closed.

Sheer terror would not allow her to remain in that position for long. If she was going to die, she must face it with her eyes open. And she thought about dying a great deal in those next few seconds.

She twisted away from Mitch's shoulder but kept her head down, looking wildly about. She saw a gaping hole appear above the doorframe as the wall wrenched violently; she saw the light fixture drop to the floor in a spray of sparks and glass.

Mitch's arm was still around her shoulders, his hand against the side of her face, and when the fixture fell he pressed her head against his shoulder again, protecting her. Diana wanted to throw her arms around him and bury herself in the shelter of his body, to cling to him as her last defense in a world gone mad, to drown in his strength. But there was no room for her to move, and she wound her fingers so tightly around his that her hand went numb. *I'm glad it's you, Mitch,* she thought. *If this is the end, I'm glad I'm with you....*

A hundred things went through her mind, and all so quickly that, even in the preternatural slow motion in which the cataclysm seemed to be unfolding, she could only focus on a few, oddly random, ideas.

She wished she hadn't lied about Japan; she had never been in a quake in Japan, she had never been in anything like this. She thought about her house. Their house, hers and Mitch's, the house she had been so willing to leave behind and now would never see again. She thought about the things she hadn't told him. She thought about all the things she hadn't done. And most of them involved Mitch.

Something slammed against the top of the desk over their heads; there was the sound of splintering wood and the top drawer sagged. Mitch's hand pressed against her face again, shielding her eyes from the rain of dust and wood slivers. Diana could feel his breath, hot and ragged against her opposite cheek, and she wanted to turn her face to his, to cover his mouth with hers and draw his breath inside her and let that be their last memory. She couldn't move. She could only watch helplessly as the world collapsed around them.

If she lived another century, she would never be able to describe the power of these, the most singular, important seconds of her life. The noise was perhaps the worst part. It blotted out everything else, even her own thoughts. It went on and on, roaring and thundering, crashing and cracking and rumbling, making it sound as though the world really were coming to an end.

Then it was over.

The shaking stopped, the roaring faded away. The stillness was absolute. The silence echoed. Diana did not move. She stayed buried in Mitch's arms, and that was where she intended to remain forever.

But the silence, as sweet as it was, was actually filled with sounds. The gush of water from a broken pipe. A sharp metallic clang as something, loosened by the quake, finally dropped. An occasional random pop or the muffled crackle of a broken electrical wire. Mitch's breathing, harsh and erratic. Her own breath, sounding strangely like sobs.

It was over. And she couldn't stay hidden forever.

Slowly, Diana lifted her head. She made herself move away from Mitch, unwinding her hand from his, inching out from under the shelter of the desk. He followed closely.

The wreckage was so thick that she was only able to move a few feet away from the desk before her path was blocked. She got to her feet on legs that were so shaky she was uncertain they would support her. She looked at the destruction around her for a long time, and the shock was so complete, the horror so overwhelming, that she couldn't even absorb it, much less react.

Not one piece of furniture remained standing. The window on the west wall had blown outward and the draperies sagged limply over the hole. Spiderweb cracks adorned the walls. A thick film of dust and crumbled Sheetrock lay over everything and was still drifting through the air, irritating Diana's lungs when she tried to draw a deep breath.

In the center of the room, suspended almost perpendicular and surrounded by a pile of broken boards, cables and unidentifiable rubble, was a bed. Its mattress was askew, its headboard missing, the bedclothes scattered. It did not belong to the Oleander Suite. It had come from the room above.

"My God." Diana's voice was flat, emotionless.

Mitch stood beside her, very close. She turned slowly to him. His expression was stunned and blank, and as uncomprehending as she felt inside.

He moved his eyes very slowly over the scene before them once again, and then looked back to her. His voice was hoarse, his breathing still uneven. "Okay," he said. "You can blame me for the riot in the lobby. The bomb was my fault. But, baby..." He moved his eyes over the room one more time in disbelief. "I swear to God, I had nothing to do with this."

Diana knew he was trying to make her smile. That he would do so, in the middle of all this—having escaped death by a hairbreadth for the second time that day—was so bizarre, so insane, so uniquely, typically Mitch, that Diana wanted to burst into tears of sheer relief and joy. She had never loved him more than she did at that moment.

She hadn't the emotional strength either to smile or cry. She could only stand and look at him mutely as his hand closed around hers and he took a cautious step forward.

Chapter Twelve

Diana pulled back, suddenly gripped by a wave of horror so intense its effect was almost paralyzing.

"No," she said. "Wait. What are you doing? Where are you going?"

"I'm getting out of here. Come on, help me clear a path to the door."

She stood there shaking her head. The thought of leaving this room, of venturing into the outside where nothing was safe, where they didn't know what they'd find, was for that moment incomprehensible. "No. We have to stay here. That's what they always say— stay where you are. The rescue teams . . ."

"*What* rescue teams?"

Incredulity and impatience crossed his dust-streaked face, and Diana noticed for the first time a small cut on his forehead, streaked with dried blood.

"Who says that?" he demanded. "Honey, I don't know what emergency-response manuals you've been reading, but we're not going to stay here and let this building fall down around us. Come on, give me a hand.''

He started to turn his attention to the rubble that was blocking their path, but Diana didn't move. Her eyes were fixed on the ragged hole in the ceiling through which the bed had fallen. Even as she stared, another piece of plaster loosened itself and tumbled through the opening. As hard as she tried, she could not picture herself taking another step forward.

Mitch glanced back at her, and he must have seen something on her face that caused his own expression to soften. His tone was a fraction gentler as he said, ''Honey, we've got to get out of here before the first aftershock hits, you know that. There are other people out there, probably worse off than we are. We have to move.''

She knew he was right. Of course he was right. But his words struck her in that moment as symbolic of their entire marriage. There was Mitch, rushing head-long into action without a thought for the consequences; there was Diana, clinging to home and hearth even when it was the wrong thing to do.

She set her jaw and stepped forward, bending to move a clutter of splintered Sheetrock and broken boards out of the way. ''Watch for hot wires,'' she said. ''You don't know what's under this mess.''

After a moment, Mitch grinned. "Grace under pressure, sweetheart," he said. "One of the first things I admired about you."

Diana met his eyes and almost managed a smile. By the time they had cleared a path to the door, they could hear sirens through the open window, very far away. They could hear voices in the hall, some panicked and hysterical, some weak and injured. And they could smell smoke. They could not tell whether it was coming from outside the building or inside the room, whether it was a serious blaze or a series of small sputtering fires. But they both knew that more people died in the fires that were the aftermath of an earthquake than in the quake itself. Diana no longer had any desire to remain behind, trapped in the room.

The door was half-open, twisted on its hinges so that there was a gap at the top that grew narrower toward the floor, where the door was pinned in place by the sofa, which seemed in turn to be supported by the bed that had fallen through the ceiling.

"This should be interesting," Mitch said.

Now, there was no mistaking the faint haze of smoke that was seeping in from the hall. They might escape being buried alive in the room only to choke to death in the hall.

Mitch looked at Diana. They both looked at the door.

"I'll go first," Mitch offered.

"Don't be absurd. I weigh less than you do. I have a better chance of getting up there and seeing what's on the other side."

"You'll *be* on the other side before you can see it!"

"At least I won't send the whole thing tumbling down, trapping us both—"

"If it's going to fall, I'd rather know it now—"

"Mitch, we're wasting time."

The set of his jaw was angry and his eyes flashed frustration, but he knew she was right. "What if what you find on the other side is fire?" he demanded.

And she replied, "Then we know."

The knot in his jaw tightened another fraction. "Damn it, Diana," he muttered. "I hate it when you're right."

Diana turned away, gingerly testing her weight with one foot on the sofa. Mitch stretched over to hold her waist.

"Okay, I've got you. See if you can brace your hand on the wall.... Got it?"

"I've got it." Diana straightened as much as she could, angling her body against the door. The sofa shifted beneath her, and she heard Mitch's sharp intake of breath.

"Watch it now. Can you see anything?"

"No..." Carefully she gripped the top of the door, easing one leg through the opening.

"Watch where you put your hand. There's a nail..."

Diana tried not to think what would happen if the aftershock hit now. If the door collapsed.

She drew one last breath of the relatively smoke-free inner-room air, and swung the other leg through the opening. She felt herself begin to slide almost immediately and knew she would not be able to control her descent. She let herself drop.

It was a short fall and she landed on her feet. The smoke was not as bad as it had looked at first. Through the haze, she could see figures and what appeared to be the source of the smoke—a small blaze near the bank of elevators. A woman was sobbing, a man was shouting in a tone of near hysteria, "Just be calm! Everybody be calm!"

Diana turned to call, "Mitch!"

But he was already squeezing through the opening, wriggling a little to free his shoulders before he dropped to the floor.

Diana ran for the fire extinguisher, breaking the glass with her shoe. The alarm bell, operated by battery backup, shrilled in her ear, and there was something chillingly ironic about that: the alarm that no one would answer.

Mitch grabbed the fire extinguisher from her. "I'll take care of it!" he shouted. "You see about the others!"

Diana nodded, coughing, and stumbled as she hurried back the way she had come. Mitch caught her arm to steady her and their eyes met. It was only a second, a brief squeeze of his fingers, a moment of mutual reassurance and strength, but it was enough. When each moment they shared might well be their last, it was more than enough.

He ran toward the small fire and Diana turned back the way she had come. There were four suites and four double rooms on the third floor. Desperately she tried to remember how many of them were occupied.

"There's a fire!" a woman shrilled, very close to her face. "Can't you hear the alarm? We have to get out of here!"

Diana caught the woman by the shoulders as she tried to push by. "It's okay!" she assured her, struggling to remember the woman's name. "Someone went to put it out. Just calm down, Mrs...." Cambell, Cray, Camp... "Cannon!" That was it. They had checked in yesterday; they were on their honeymoon en route to Hawaii; Diana had ordered a bottle of champagne for their room....

All that went through her head in a fraction of a second even as she spoke. "Are you hurt? Where's your husband?"

The authority in Diana's voice must have reached the woman because some of the hysteria left her eyes, and she seemed to focus for a moment. "We were— were going out for dinner. I was dressing and he—went down to wait in the lounge. He was going to come back up at seven, but—'' She burst into tears.

Diana guided her back against the wall. "Here. Just sit down, stay here and don't move. We'll find your husband. I'm sure he's fine."

Diana wasn't sure of anything of the kind but she had no energy to spare on fearing the worst and no time to spend comforting the frightened woman.

She did not know how long she stumbled through that haze of smoke and terror, coughing, eyes streaming, repeating meaningless phrases of comfort and reassurance as hands clutched at her and voices called. It seemed like a lifetime.

She was at the window at the end of the corridor where most of the smoke seemed to have accumulated, trying to knock a pane out of the safety glass.

"Stand back," Mitch said.

Using the fire extinguisher as a battering ram, he smashed the glass outward in several places. Almost immediately, a gust of fresh air began to dissipate the smoke, bringing with it sounds from below—sounds of shock and panic, wailing sirens, car alarms, fire alarms, burglar alarms. Pandemonium. Mitch stood at the window for a long moment, looking out.

Diana took an uncertain step toward him, afraid to look for herself, but afraid not to ask. "Mitch? How bad?"

In the first moment he looked at her, he almost did not have to answer. She saw it in the dull disbelief that filled his eyes. With a breath he brought his expression under control, but he didn't try to lie to her. "Pretty bad. Still . . ." He looked around uneasily. "I think we're better off down there than up here. How many people have you found?"

"Four. Most of them were in the corridor when the quake struck. A couple of them are hurt, but no one very badly. Only two rooms and one suite—plus yours—on this floor were occupied, so that should be everyone. But we should check the rooms anyway."

The surge of admiration in his eyes was swift and genuine.

"The fire's out," he said. "But there are people stuck in the elevator. I need somebody to help me pry open the doors."

"Mr. Feldman's arm is broken," Diana said. "Mr. Hanes hurt his back—he can barely walk. Mrs. Cannon and Mrs. Hanes won't be much help to you. So I guess I volunteer."

He smiled. "I would've picked you anyway. What can we use as a crowbar?"

Someone plucked at Diana's skirt. "Are the elevators working? Are you going to fix the elevators?" And someone else demanded, "What's the matter with this damn city, anyway? How could they let something like this happen?"

It was shock, Diana knew, but not the physical kind. It was the kind of total disorientation that comes from being abruptly thrust into the unknown, of drowning in turmoil, of simply not knowing what to do. Diana was familiar with that sensation. It sometimes seemed it had become part of her life-style from the moment she started living with Mitch.

Mitch found a narrow piece of pipe from the pile of rubble near the stairway and handed it to Diana. "I'm going to try to pull the doors open a little. When I do, see if you can wedge that in there."

Diana followed him as they picked their way through the litter of the hallway toward the elevators. "What if it's too far down for us to reach?" she asked tightly.

"We have to find out."

"What if—" she had to force the next words "—people are hurt?"

They had been lucky so far, but there was no way to guess what they might find in the elevator.

"Then we'd better hurry, hadn't we?"

"Maybe you were wrong. Maybe there isn't anybody."

But he hadn't been wrong. She could hear the voices, faint and muffled by thick steel, as soon as they reached the elevator doors.

Please, Diana thought, *let everyone be all right. . . .*

The end of the pipe was too thick to fit between the doors. Mitch managed to get the tips of his fingers into the small space and, bracing his feet, he pulled back. Diana put the pipe down, close at hand, and moved in quickly, sliding her fingers in the space beneath his and adding her strength to his.

"Can I tell you something?"

Mitch's voice was tight with effort, his face already growing red. Diana knew the feeling; she pulled back with all her might and the door barely budged an inch.

"What?" Her reply was an explosion of breath.

"That's . . . the first thing that attracted me to you. Your fearlessness. And I bet . . . you thought it was your legs."

For just a moment Diana let her concentration falter, and she stared at him. "Fearless?" Quickly, she turned back to the job at hand. "Is that what you thought?"

A fine sweat had broken out on Mitch's face. The muscles in his neck bulged. Diana thought her own fingers would break off at the tips, and her shoulders were growing numb. But as she redoubled her efforts, she thought the doors actually parted a fraction.

"Okay!" gasped Mitch. "I've got it—I can hold it! Get the pipe in there!"

Diana hurried to wedge the pipe in. It took some doing, and she glanced anxiously at Mitch more than once. When at last she had the pipe firmly taking the weight of the doors, Mitch released his grip and shook out his arms, cursing.

He put his hands next to hers on the pipe and used his body for leverage. The doors slowly began to part.

"Weren't you?"

"What?"

"Fearless."

Diana didn't look at him. She didn't dare take her attention off the steady pressure she was exerting on the pipe. "That's so typical of you, Mitch." Her voice was tight, breathless with exertion. "You only see what suits you."

"Is that a fact?"

His sweaty hands slipped on the pipe and his shoulder hit the door. He swore. Diana moved quickly to take up the slack, but the door slid almost closed again before Mitch regained his grip.

Diana's heart lurched as someone called out from inside the shaft. "It's okay!" Mitch called back. "Hold on!"

To Diana he said, "You want to explain to me just why it would suit me to be attracted to a strong, fearless Amazon like you?"

"Strong women don't require anything from you. You don't have to do anything. Makes your life easy. And you like it that way."

"Yeah, you made it easy, all right. Life with you was a damn cakewalk. And you needed me less than any woman I've ever known."

Diana pressed her lips together, applying strength she did not even know she had to the metal pipe. "I needed you, Mitch," she said, her voice low with strain. "You just never noticed."

Mitch was standing beside her and a little behind and she couldn't see his face. But she felt the contraction of his muscles as he, too, gave one last mighty pull on the pipe, forcing the doors apart almost a foot. Simultaneously, they dropped the pipe. Diana's muscles were shaking.

Mitch came around to grab one of the doors with his hands, opening it wider, and then their eyes met for a moment. He wanted to say more, she could see it. And there was no surprise—on his part or hers—that they should be having this conversation in this time and place; it even seemed oddly appropriate. Because during the last few moments, they had shared more honesty with each other than they had during their entire marriage.

Diana dropped to her knees and tried to see inside the shaft. "I need more room," she told Mitch. "Not enough light. See if you can—"

Mitch pulled hard and the door slid open unexpectedly. Diana found herself kneeling on the edge of an elevator shaft gazing down into what seemed to be an endless abyss. It wasn't, of course. The elevator itself was not even half a story below her, but she could see beyond it, dusty specks of swirling light on either side, a maze of swaying cables and pulsing metal beams. And even as she stared, frozen in place, she felt herself falling, turning head over heels like Alice tumbling through the looking glass....

Mitch took her shoulders and pulled her gently back from the edge. She was breathing hard, and cold perspiration glazed her face.

"I'll take it from here, babe," Mitch said.

She didn't pretend to protest. Even though she no longer was looking down, her head swam. She suppressed a shudder as she muttered, "Fearless."

He glanced at her. "That doesn't count."

"Is everybody okay down there?" he shouted into the shaft. "Anybody hurt?"

"We're okay!" a male voice came in reply. "How does it look up there?"

"I don't see anything broken," Mitch called back. "I think I can get you out. How many?"

"Two." A hesitance. "DeSalvo?"

Mitch looked startled, then his face broke into a grin. "Harold?"

The other man sounded resigned. "Why am I not surprised?"

"There's a trapdoor. I think I can open it from this side. Hold on."

He turned away from the shaft. Diana caught his arm. Her throat was dry, her stomach hollow. "Mitch. You're not going down there?"

Understanding softened his expression briefly. "It's no big deal, babe, just a few feet. I could jump down, but I won't," he assured her. "Come on, help me get that fire hose over here."

Her fingers tightened on his arm. The thought of Mitch descending into that black pit left her almost paralyzed with terror. If the cable snapped... If the elevator shifted or could not support his weight... If the aftershock came... If he slipped...

He read it all in her eyes. His answer was to lean forward and kiss her lightly on the lips. "Come on," he said softly. "Give me a hand."

The fire hose was in a case beneath the portable extinguisher they had already taken, and when the survivors saw them returning for it, a mild panic erupted.

"A fire? Is there another fire?"

"We've got to get out of here, doesn't anybody realize that?"

"My husband—"

"The fire door's locked, I checked! That means we're trapped—"

"A doctor! We've got to have a doctor!"

Diana raised her voice to be heard, but none of the wild-edged terror she was feeling was reflected in it.

"Will everyone please just try to *calm down?* The worst thing you can do now is panic!"

Somewhat to her amazement, the clamor died down. Frightened, smoke-streaked faces turned toward her, some anxious, some defiant, all helpless.

"We're going to get out of here," she went on firmly. "We're working on that now. But we have to work together. If those of you who aren't badly hurt would check the rooms on this floor to make certain no one is trapped inside, it would be a big help. Mrs. Cannon, maybe you could start at this end of the hall."

It was a logical choice; Mrs. Cannon was the only person who had no one to take care of. Giving her something to do was the best way to postpone incipient hysteria. Gulping back her shuddering sobs, the woman got to her feet.

As Diana had hoped, at least one of the men was shamed by a woman's being asked to help while he sat idly by. Mr. Feldman, his broken arm stabilized in a sling improvised from his tie, pushed to his feet. "I'll help."

"Nice call, princess," Mitch murmured, shouldering a heavy coil of hose. "I knew I brought you along for something."

Diana unwound more canvas hose from the hook as he moved back toward the elevators. "Is this strong enough to hold your weight?" she worried.

"Of course it is. They do it on television all the time."

"Damn it, Mitch, this is not one of your novels!"

"Hey, no kidding. Even I couldn't have dreamed up this nightmare."

Diana stopped where she was, squeezing her eyes closed for a moment of uncontrolled emotion, clenching her teeth. "I *hate* it when you do that! Always playing the hero, wading in waist deep—and loving every minute of it! God, Mitch, you *could* have made this up. It's perfect for you—your own starring role!"

Mitch's expression, when he looked at her, was gentle and understanding.

"Why don't you go help the others?" he said. "I can take care of this myself."

"No," she said sharply. "I'll stay. I'll help." And she drew a breath. "Just—damn it, Mitch, be careful."

He smiled and caressed her cheek in a brief teasing gesture that left her skin tingling and her heart pounding with the simple affirmation of life and warmth. "Yes, Mom."

Together, they looped the hose around two sofa legs. Mitch tested its strength by tugging firmly, then stepped to the edge of the shaft.

Diana moved behind him and picked up the slack, holding on tightly and bracing her feet. Mitch smiled, but she met his eyes defiantly. They both knew if the hose slipped nothing she could do would save him.

"Don't you dare fall, Mitch."

"Don't worry," he answered. "I'll be back."

The look in his eyes caught in her heart. "I just realized, I'm not finished with you yet."

Using the hose like a rappelling rope, Mitch stepped into the shaft.

Chapter Thirteen

It did not take any particular courage for Mitch to lower himself into the elevator shaft. It was simply a matter of identifying what had to be done and figuring out how to do it, and he did not consider the rescue either difficult or dangerous.

But for Diana to stand above and watch, looking down into the face of the thing she feared the most and holding on to the slack end of the canvas hose as though her frail strength could actually make a difference—that, to Mitch, was the purest demonstration of simple heroism he had ever known.

That, he realized suddenly, was why he loved her. Not because she was strong, not because she was brave or smart or beautiful or heroic, although she was all those things. But because of this sense of twoness, of knowing she was always there, holding the rope, despite her personal fears and whether she wanted to be there or not. Because from the moment he had met her, something had fused between them, and he had known even then that he would never be alone again. He could say goodbye to her a hundred times, leave her behind a thousand, but he would never be alone. Despite what she wanted, despite what he wanted, they were a team. It was that simple.

It was not as simple to release the two men trapped below, yet Mitch succeeded. Harold helped him over the edge just as Greg Cannon, the first man he had freed, rushed into the arms of his distraught wife. Mitch met Diana's eyes, still breathing hard from the exercise.

"I do like a happy ending," he said.

Diana's face was pale under its filmy coating of dust, her eyes dark with strain. But she smiled weakly in response.

"It's not exactly a happy ending yet," Harold said grimly. He looked at Diana. "Does this hotel have a disaster plan?"

"Of course." It was simply that, in a disaster this big, the plan seemed very low on the list of priorities. "There's a storage closet at the other end of the hall with radios and walkie-talkies. Someone will be manning a central command station and they'll have information and instructions for us."

"Sounds like it'd be a smart move to get one of those walkie-talkies," Mitch suggested. "Before we go barging into something that might put us in worse shape than we are already.''

Harold nodded agreement and Diana looked at Mitch in some surprise.

"That's the first time I've ever known you to do the smart thing," she said.

He hesitated, looking a little surprised himself, even uncomfortable. "It's also the first time I've lived through a car bomb and an earthquake in one day. A guy's gotta wonder how many more breaks he's got left."

That made Diana smile. "I'll get the radios. Somebody should check the stairwell. I thought I heard someone say the door was locked."

"Jammed, more likely." Harold looked worried. "I'll check it out. It might be something we can move."

"Good idea." Mitch looked at Harold. "Say, what is your real name, anyway?"

The other man looked for a moment as though he'd prefer to ignore the question. There was a note of defiance in his tone as he answered, "Rupert. Rupert Jones."

Mitch was silent for a beat. "Right. See what you can do about keeping the situation under control here, will you, Harold?"

Diana was halfway to the closet when Mitch caught up with her.

"I don't need your help," she said. "It'll be faster if I go alone."

"See? There you go."

"What?"

"You don't need me. You never did."

"Oh, Mitch, for heaven's sake, this is hardly the time—"

He caught one shoulder and turned her around. "We've just been through a major earthquake," he said very calmly. "We're trapped on the third floor of a building with no elevators and a blocked staircase, sitting under several hundred tons of concrete and steel that could decide to let go at any minute. There's at least one major fire above us and probably half a dozen smaller ones, as well. I'll tell you the truth, babe—it looks to me if there ever was a time to clear the air between us, it's now."

He saw the small muscles of her throat constrict as she swallowed, but her gaze did not waver. Her hands slowly tightened into fists at her sides as she said, "I loved you from the first minute I set eyes on you, Mitch DeSalvo, and I never stopped loving you, not once in all these years. I nearly died of loving you. I've never wanted anyone or anything as much as I wanted you, or hurt as much as I hurt for you, and if you think any of that makes a difference now—"

The aftershock hit swiftly and intensely, a thunderclap that went on too long, heaving the floor and shaking the walls. Diana was in Mitch's arms, though whether she had been thrown there or had run to him, she didn't know.

His arms were so tight they crushed off her breath, and her arms ached with holding him, but neither of them noticed, not really, as the ceiling cracked overhead and chunks of plaster fell like hail. They sank to the floor against the wall, Mitch shielding her with his body, Diana trying to protect his head with her arms.

When it was over, they didn't move for a long time. They stayed there, crouched against the wall, clinging to each other and listening to the sounds of each other's harsh, ragged breathing, drinking it in.

Then, on a long exhalation of breath, Mitch said, "Baby, do you ever get the feeling God is trying to tell us something?"

Diana pushed away from him unsteadily, though it was the last thing she wanted to do. His arms seemed to be the only solid thing in a world made of quicksand.

"I'm not sure I want to know what it is," she said shakily.

Once again they had been lucky. Dust still choked the air. The ceiling looked like the open belly of some prehistoric creature, with its exposed network of twisted pipes and sagging wires. The floor was knee-deep in rubble in some places, but neither of them had been hurt. If that was the worst of the aftershock, they just might survive.

Or it could be only the beginning.

"Seems to me every time we get ready to call it quits, we get hit with another shock," Mitch said. "Maybe He's trying to tell us to stop wasting our time and face the fact that we're stuck together."

Diana's heart, already pounding, caught in her chest for half a beat, then resumed. She glanced at him but was determined not to let it show. "Or maybe He's trying to tell us that we're the authors of our own destruction."

She started to stand up but he held her. He looked at her, and the world stood still. Diana wanted more than anything in her life to know what he was going to say next.

"Hey!" somebody called. "Anybody hurt? You two okay?"

Mitch turned away from her to shout back, "Okay! How about back there?"

"Okay! We're going on!"

Diana braced her hand against his arm to stand. "You should go. They might need you."

Mitch stood up, brushing a shower of paint chips and plaster dust from his hair as though it were the most normal everyday occurrence. "Tell me something. Before the quake, as you were getting ready to leave, you stopped, and you started to say something. What was it?"

Diana drew a breath to answer but somehow the words wouldn't come. It was so long ago. A lifetime ago, a century ago. Did any of it matter now?

Nonetheless, she heard herself saying, "What was the message you left on my machine?"

In his eyes, she saw the same kind of hesitance, of uncertainty. Like Diana, he was willing to go so far, but neither was ready to step over the invisible line that had been between them almost as long as they could remember.

He turned and bent to clear a pile of broken molding and shattered plaster that blocked their path. "Tell you what, sweetie. Let's get out of here and you can listen to it for yourself."

Diana moved to help him, kicking chunks of plaster aside with her foot. "If it's still there."

"The message?"

"The house."

There was an almost infinitesimal pause in his movements. "What difference does it make? You're on your way to New Orleans, anyway."

That struck her like a knife. She did not even try to analyze why, after all they had just survived and had yet to endure, that careless, insensitive comment should make her so angry.

She had bent to move a narrow board out of the way; now she tossed it against the wall so hard that it cracked. "Do you think that's what I want?"

"Hell, Di, I never could figure out what you want." There was angry tension in his voice, too, and he didn't look at her. "All I ever came up with was that whatever it was, it wasn't me."

"You know that's not true!"

"You wanted tuxedos and literary teas and tasteful inscriptions in leather-bound volumes. What you got was overflowing ashtrays and postage due."

"Damn it, Mitch! Do you really think those things were important to me?"

"How was I even supposed to guess what a woman like you wanted? You were just too different from anything I'd ever known, Diana," he said quietly. "And I wasn't used to failing—but after a while, it just got too hard to try."

The quake had not rocked Diana as much as hearing those words from the man she thought she knew so well. The one thing she had never guessed. For a moment she couldn't speak.

She pressed the heel of her hand against her forehead, blotting the sticky film of perspiration and dust. In a small voice, she said, "You weren't like anyone I'd ever known, either, Mitch. You were such a street-tough, hard-talking man... such a *hero* all the time. I'd never known anybody like you. The things you did without thinking twice were things I couldn't even imagine doing."

She looked at him, trying to keep the sorrow and desperation out of her voice but wanting him to understand. After all this time, having come so far, please let him understand....

"Oh, Mitch, don't you see? The only thing I've ever really been afraid of in my whole life is falling. All I wanted was someone who would catch me if I fell, and you were never there."

Mitch looked at her for a long and sober moment. Then he said, "How do you know? How do you know I wouldn't have caught you? You never gave me a chance. You never fell. You never even stumbled."

Diana shook her head slowly. "I was afraid."

"You didn't trust me."

She thought she had never heard greater sadness in anyone's voice. But she couldn't lie to him. "No."

For another moment he held her gaze, then he turned to lead the way down the hall.

Half the ceiling had come down in front of the storage closet; it was blocked by a waist-high pile of broken boards and twisted insulation. Without exchanging a word, they moved forward to clear the door.

Without looking at her, Mitch asked, "So why take the job in New Orleans if you didn't want to go?"

That was hard. But she owed him the truth, even though she couldn't quite meet his eyes when she said it. "I only stayed here because . . . I knew you'd keep coming back. The house . . . as much as I love it, it was only home to me because you made it home. Because that was where the dream almost came true."

And then she looked at him, helpless beneath the hurt and loss. "Tonight, when I knew it was really over, I knew I couldn't stay here without you, and be reminded for the rest of my life of what I almost had."

She shook her head slowly. "That was really the trouble with us, wasn't it, Mitch? We just had different dreams. I wanted the home and hearth and the patter of little feet, and you wanted . . ." She tried to smile. "Moscow."

He had lifted a wide board halfway to his waist; at her words he froze in midmovement, raising his eyes to her. "No." He tossed the board aside and straightened up. "The trouble with us is we're too much alike. The house, the rose garden, seven kids lined up at suppertime with faces scrubbed . . . that's where I came from. And the hell of it is, I've spent my whole life trying to get back there." His voice was tight. "Of course, I didn't realize it until I'd already lost the woman who could make it come true. We had the same dream all the time, princess, we were just chasing it down in different directions."

"Oh, Mitch." An enormous, bone-weary defeat drained through her. "Why did it take us so long to realize that?" And why did he have to tell her now, when it was too late?

Mitch had no answer. He turned back to the doorway, which was clear enough now to allow the door to open almost a foot. Diana squeezed through.

"Can you get me more light?"

"This is as far as it'll open without bringing who knows what crashing down on our heads."

Diana groped blindly in the dimness until her hands skated over a large metal box in a corner near the back of the closet. She dragged it out and maneuvered it through the door opening.

"Bingo," Mitch said. He was sitting on the floor with the open box by the time Diana squeezed back out of the closet. "Flashlights, first-aid kit, radio..." He picked up the small radio, turned it on, then flung it on the floor in disgust. "With dead batteries."

Diana had the walkie-talkie and switched it on. "Hello, Command Center... This is Diana Moore on the third floor. Is anybody there? Come in, please."

Silence.

"Command Center, are you there? Security, anybody... Come on guys, we've got troubles here."

Nothing.

"Batteries?" Mitch asked.

She held the unit close enough for him to hear the static. Feeling hollow inside, she replied, "There's no one there."

"That doesn't mean anything," Mitch said quickly, taking the unit from her. "Their receiver could have been damaged or they haven't had time to set up yet or..."

"Or no one's there." Her voice was dull with the weight of what that could mean. "Elise, Mr. Severenson, Carla... I told Elise to go home. If she left, she would have been caught on the freeway...."

Mitch gripped her arm. "Come on, Di, there's no point in that kind of thinking."

But the horror went over her in waves and wouldn't stop. "All those people in the restaurant and lounge... Friday night, our busiest night..."

"Stop it." His grip tightened and he pulled her to her feet, holding the emergency box under his other arm. "Those people were on the first floor. They had a chance to make it to the street. We're the ones in trouble here."

Diana knew he was right. She had to get hold of herself. She couldn't waste energy on what she couldn't change, not when it would take everything she had just to survive the next few hours.

Still holding her arm, Mitch turned back the way they had come.

"Mr. Severenson said there was an article about you in the *New York Times*."

He didn't look back. "I can tell you're impressed."

"That's what I always liked about you, you know. You're not impressed by anything," she said.

Then he glanced at her. "Wrong, babe. I was impressed by you. A lot."

Diana hesitated. "It's starting to sound as though we spent an awful lot of time being impressed by each other, but not much time doing anything about it."

She stopped, and he turned to look at her.

"Mitch," she said. "Before—when I started to leave, before the quake—what I was going to say was..." She swallowed hard to clear her throat of a sudden thickness. "I just wanted...I just wanted to make love with you, one more time."

The slow smile that softened his taut, weary features was more soothing than a caress. It filled her with light and hope and the warm quiet strength that was the essence of Mitch.

"I sure do wish you'd spoken up sooner, sweetie."

"Hey, DeSalvo!"

They turned to see the man Mitch called Harold hurrying toward them.

"Anything on the radio?"

Mitch looked back at Diana for one brief moment of tenderness and regret, then moved forward to meet the other man. "No radio, nothing on the house system. We've got a first-aid kit, though."

Diana followed more slowly as Harold said, "The good news is that last shock loosened whatever was blocking the fire door. I think with one more man we can get it open. We heard people in the stairwell not long ago so the passage must be clear."

"You got it."

Mitch passed the emergency box to Diana and moved away.

WHY THERE WERE only three flashlights in an emergency kit designed to serve a whole floor, Diana could not begin to guess. She was only grateful that they all worked.

They closed the fire door behind them; it was the only sensible thing to do. The eight of them stepped into the hot, smoke- and dust-filled tunnel of the stairwell. Harold, in the lead, took one of the flashlights; Greg Cannon, in the middle, had another; and Mitch, bringing up the rear, had the last. The best they could do was use the lights to make certain no one missed a step and fell; not even Harold could see what lay before them.

Diana counted the steps. She had never before realized there were so many steps between stories. Three floors. Only three floors. But there was certainly no

guarantee that they would be able to get out of the
stairwell even if they reached the ground level.

Please, she prayed, *just let us get out of here. Just
let us....*

And when the slow-moving line of bodies in front
of her stopped, so did her heart.

"The second floor door is hot," Harold called.
"The smoke gets thicker up ahead."

Very close behind, Mitch murmured, "Okay, babe,
no malingering. If that door is hot to the touch, it
could blow at any minute. I'd rather not be behind it
when it does."

Diana wasn't sure she took a breath until they were
past the door, descending the last flight to safety
through a mist of smoky darkness.

It might have been the illusion of privacy offered by
the shallow depth at which Mitch's beam of light
penetrated the darkness. It might have been his close-
ness, so near she could feel his breath on her hair,
making it easy to pretend there were only the two of
them in the stairwell. But suddenly she had to talk to
him; there was so much to say to him, a lifetime of
things to say and not nearly enough time in which to
say them all.

Oddly, the only place she could think of to start was
by saying, "I read your books." Her voice sounded
rushed, a little breathless. "All of them."

If he felt any surprise, he didn't show it. "Then you know the hero always gets out alive." The touch of his hand on the small of her back was steady and reassuring. "And so does the woman he loves."

Diana held on tightly to the metal handrail as she made her descent. What she really wanted to do was turn and fling her arms around Mitch and hold on tight and not move another muscle, ever. Let the world crumble to ashes around them; as long as she could hold on to him, it wouldn't matter.

"That's the difference between fiction and real life, Mitch." Her breath was still coming in short shallow gasps, more from fear than exertion. "You can't just make a happy ending by wishing it so. If you could, then..."

But she couldn't finish.

"Then what?" he prompted. "What would you wish?"

A colorful Victorian house on Russian Hill, book-lined study, crackling fire, Mitch in her arms.... If she could close her eyes and instantly transport herself anywhere in the world just by wishing, that was all she would want for the rest of her life.

And to think that once she had had it.

"What was the message, Mitch?" she demanded quietly, slowing her step only a fraction. "What did you leave on my machine?"

He hesitated, but perhaps he, too, was touched by the same urgency that had gripped Diana. They had survived so much already; even though the worst might well be behind them and safety just around the next corner, neither of them could afford to take a chance. They had used up too many of them.

And so Mitch answered in the same quiet tone, "I said I loved you, and I loved you so much I was going to let you go. I said I hoped you found somebody who was good enough for you and that I would miss you for the rest of my life."

Diana's step faltered. She couldn't help it, she stopped and turned to look at him, though she could see nothing but a shadow in the reflected light of his flashlight beam.

"You said that?" Her voice was hoarse. "You were going to let me come home to that—and you would be gone?"

There was puzzlement in his voice. "Why? What's wrong? It was the truth."

She drew a quick sharp breath to reply, then released it wordlessly. She shook her head and began moving down the steps again. "Nothing. Never mind. It doesn't make any difference now."

Mitch said, "That's the second time you've said that."

"What?"

"That it doesn't make a difference."

Diana didn't know how to reply.

They were on the first-floor landing. Diana knew it only because she had counted the steps. Almost there. Almost...

Then Mitch grabbed her, forced her up against the wall and kissed her hard. It was a kiss of triumph and defiance, of strength and determination and possession. It took Diana's breath away; it made her head spin with hope and possibilities and belief in the future; it gave her, in that one brief moment, all that she needed.

And when it was over, he still held her close against the wall, pinned with his pelvis and his thighs, the hand that did not hold the flashlight cupping her face.

"What was that for?" she gasped.

And he answered, his voice low and fierce, "Because it *does* make a difference. Because I love you and you love me and it's *got* to matter, it has to count for something. Because we may be all wrong for each other but we're miserable without each other and that's got to mean something, damn it, it *has* to."

"Mitch, I—"

When she started to turn away in confusion, his fingers tightened on her face, making her look at him. "Listen to me," he said fiercely, breathing hard. "Can't you see we belong together? You can't live without me. You have to admit it. I tried living without you, but I keep coming back here. And it's gone on long enough. This time I'm not leaving without you, do you understand that?''

It was hard to keep her voice steady, hard to keep her thoughts steady, hard to do anything at all except fling herself into his arms and pretend it could be that simple, that everything could be perfect just because they wanted it to be....

Her voice shook as she asked, ''Are you sure this is not just terror talking?''

''Yes, it is,'' he said, searching her eyes. ''Terror of losing you.''

The others were far ahead of them. ''I can see light!'' someone shouted. ''I think the door is open!''

Neither Diana nor Mitch moved. ''We can't make every dream come true, Di,'' Mitch said urgently. ''But this one we can. The house, the garden, the kids—that's *ours*. We almost lost it once but it's not too late. Marry me, Di. Say yes.''

She wanted to. She wanted to scream it, to shout it, to believe it. Trapped in a staircase in the middle of an earthquake, she knew there was nothing more important in that moment than his question, than her answer, and she wanted it to be the right one, the true one. She wanted it to be real.

Her voice was hoarse. ''We'll just make the same mistakes.''

''Maybe we won't.''

"Mitch, I want to, but . . ." But she was afraid. Afraid of failing, afraid of believing in him, afraid of losing him again.

"Then do it," he said. "Just tell me."

"I'm not—"

And once again the earth erupted beneath their feet and shuddered over their heads, once again they were thrown to their knees, clutching each other, trying to shield each other, holding on for dear life for what seemed like forever. *Too late,* Diana thought. *We had our chance and we wasted it. . . . Too late. . . .*

Then it was over and she thought perhaps it wasn't too late because Mitch was still there. But the staircase wasn't.

Two steps below where they crouched on the landing, the stairway had cracked and separated. At least four steps were missing, as though they had been simply sliced away. As Mitch played his flashlight over the scene, he picked up thick whirling smoke, crumbled concrete and naked steel supports, and, in the gap where the steps should have been, nothing but darkness, a deadly drop into the subbasement. Mitch quickly jerked the light away.

A voice came from below. "DeSalvo? You back there? You okay?"

It was a moment before Mitch responded. Diana could feel his eyes on her, but she could not drag her gaze away from the dark pit that yawned between them and safety. *Too late....*

"Yo, Harold!" Mitch called back. "No harm done! You?"

"We made it! The door's not blocked. Can you get down?"

"It might be tricky." Mitch deliberately kept his beam away from the gap in the stairwell. "But we can do it."

And to Diana he added, softly, "Can't we, babe?"

Diana couldn't even nod.

Mitch got to his feet, pulling her up with him by keeping his arm firmly around her shoulders. His voice was very calm, very steady. "This is going to be a piece of cake, sweetheart. The railing is intact. You're going to use that to swing yourself across, just like monkey bars in the playground. Just let your hands slide and don't look down. I'll be right behind you."

Diana shook her head. She tried to draw in a deep breath and began to cough. The smoke was sharper and thicker than it had been before; her eyes were watering and it was difficult to see, even with the flashlight.

"Mitch, I can't. You know I can't."

His arm tightened around her shoulders painfully. Tension crept into his voice. "Honey, I hate to point out the obvious, but we don't have a lot of choice here—or a lot of time. That last tremor must've blown off the second-story door because the atmosphere is getting pretty thick here. I don't know how much longer we're going to be able to breathe, much less see."

His voice was beginning to hoarsen with inhaled smoke, and when he drew the back of his hand across his eyes, he left a single clean swatch across his soot-darkened skin.

"Come on, baby, don't do this to me." He tried to disguise the urgency in his voice with little success. "You're bigger than this."

"I know." It was getting harder and harder to make her voice work. The smoke was only part of it. "It's just—I can't go first. I can't."

She could feel his struggle and she hated to be the cause of it, but she had no choice. And neither did he.

"Okay." He took her hand and pulled her with him down the two remaining steps. His fingers were like steel. "I'll go first. You do what I do, put your hands where I do. Stay right behind me."

Diana couldn't answer. She was looking into that great gaping emptiness that went on and on and she thought, *Is this how it ends, then? After all we've been through? Damn it, Mitch, why does it have to be like this?*

"Hey," he said sharply. "Look at me. There's nothing to see down there. Keep your eyes on me. Do what I do."

Slowly, she dragged her eyes to his. She could see the strength there, the command, and she thought, *No, not like this....*

"Reason number fifty-seven," she said softly.

"What?"

"You make me believe the impossible. Reason number fifty-seven. I'll explain it to you someday."

Some of the tight muscles around his eyes eased. "I'm counting on that," he said.

He tucked the flashlight into the belt of his jeans and put his hands on the rail. "You with me?"

Diana wiped her wet palms on her skirt, then placed her hands next to Mitch's on the rail.

"Yes," she said.

Mitch stepped off into the air.

And the rail broke.

Diana screamed and lurched backward, stumbling on the step, sprawling back against broken concrete. She heard Mitch's startled oath, saw the wild arc of the flashlight beam as Mitch's body swung out and away from Diana, suspended for one horrible moment over the gaping pit below. Diana scrambled to her feet. "*No!*" she screamed hoarsely. "Damn you, Mitch...."

And then he let go of the rail and landed on all fours safely on the other side.

Diana's head swam. She sank back against the wall, fingers pressing into the solid concrete. *Thank You, God,* she thought. *Thank You....*

When she could focus again, Mitch was getting to his feet. He had placed the flashlight on the step below him, and even through the thickening smoke she could see his effort to grin. "Fooled you," he called. "You can't get rid of me that easily."

Diana almost smiled. She wanted to smile. She called back shakily, "I always did say you had nine lives."

And then their smiles faded as they looked at each other across the abyss. "I'd give eight of them," Mitch said, "to have you on this side right now."

Now that the light was coming from the other side, Diana could see that the gap really wasn't so wide. Because of the turn the steps took, the distance between them was not a straight drop down, more of a perpendicular length, which was how Mitch had managed to land on the step instead of falling through to the basement.

"Come on, Di," he said quietly. "Your turn."

The rail remained at a ninety-degree angle away from her, touching the other wall. Even if she could have reached it, it would not have helped her reach Mitch.

"You're going to have to jump. You can do it. It looks wider than it is. It's nothing. With those legs of yours you can make it without even trying."

But it was a narrow step, and the fall would go on forever.

Diana coughed and wiped her streaming eyes. Mitch's voice grew sharper.

"Come on, Di, we haven't got all day. I can see the door from here. We're almost there."

She wanted to. Her lungs were burning, and so were her nasal passages. She drew her arm across her eyes again. Pretty soon she wouldn't be able to see at all.

"Damn it, Diana, don't you leave me here alone! We've got a life together, and I'm not going to give it up without a fight this time. Are you?"

She could see him through the smoke, backlit by the flashlight, his arms extended for her. How many more chances would they get?

"I'll catch you," he said. "For God's sake, Di, jump!"

Diana closed her eyes, and jumped.

Epilogue

The sky turned around and around as Mitch caught her up in his arms, laughing. Diana was laughing, too, beating him playfully with her fists. "Stop it, you idiot. Put me down! You're making me dizzy!"

"The day a man can't carry his bride over the threshold is the day I'll know this country is in real trouble."

"You're a nut. And you're going to drop me!"

He looked down at her. "Have I ever?"

"No," she answered softly.

Lifting her arms, she encircled his neck, bringing his mouth down to hers.

Three months after the quake, the city had almost completely recovered. It had taken most of that time for Mitch and Diana, working together and with painstaking effort, to repair the damage that had been done to their house on Russian Hill. Tonight they were hosting their first open house to celebrate the completion of the work. That morning they had awakened in their newly decorated bedroom and decided it would be appropriate if they were married for the occasion.

The bride wore a white silk suit, much like the one she had worn the first day Mitch had seen her, and carried a bouquet of white daisies. The groom wore jeans, running shoes, and a striped cutaway coat over a white T-shirt. It was a quiet ceremony held at city hall, attended by Elise and the man who would forevermore be known simply as Harold.

They had reached the front door, and reluctantly Diana ended the kiss, reaching down to turn the knob. With a flourish, Mitch swept her over the threshold and into the bright, sunny foyer.

The stained glass had, amazingly, survived with only a few cracks. The most striking change was the removal of the spiral staircase. The foyer had been enlarged to accommodate a more traditional stair system, painted white with a gleaming oak banister, surrounded by windows and forming the perfect showcase for the chandelier overhead. Together they had designed the room and together they had completed it.

Mitch could not resist stopping now for a moment to admire the results. "You know," he said, "this was a hell of a good idea."

Diana looped her arm around his neck again, smiling. "That," she said, "remains to be seen."

His eyes sparked amusement. "I was talking about the staircase."

"I wasn't."

"I know."

He kissed her again and when he lifted his face, she was breathless and flushed, dazed as always with the chemistry that flared between them. It never got old. Never.

"I stand corrected," she said breathlessly. "I think I've seen all I need to."

And he grinned as he murmured, "Baby, you ain't seen nothing yet."

Holding her tightly against his chest, he carried her up the stairs.

Where do you find hot Texas nights, smooth Texas charm and dangerously sexy cowboys?

COWBOYS AND CABERNET

Raise a glass—Texas style!

Tyler McKinney is out to prove a Texas ranch is the perfect place for a vineyard. Vintner Ruth Holden thinks Tyler is too stubborn, too impatient, too... Texas. And far too difficult to resist!

CRYSTAL CREEK reverberates with the exciting rhythm of Texas. Each story features the rugged individuals who live and love in the Lone Star State. And each one ends with the same invitation...

Y'ALL COME BACK... REAL SOON!

Don't miss *COWBOYS AND CABERNET* by Margot Dalton. Available in April wherever Harlequin books are sold.